THE BARROW LOVER

PATRICK TODOROFF

Patrick Todoroff

THE BARROW LOVER

© 2014 Patrick Todoroff

Print Version ISBN: 978-0-9896361-5-5

This is a work of fiction. Names, characters, places and incidents either are the product of the author's imagination or are used fictionally, and any resemblance to actual persons, living or dead, events, or locales is entirely coincidental.

A man wrapped in himself is a small package indeed.

Eternal gratitude to my family
and friends
for bringing me beyond myself.

Not All of Them

"The dead are patient," my mother used to say. "They can't come back to us, but they know in their bones we all go to them, sooner or later."

It wasn't true, what my mother said. Not that we don't all die; we do. No escaping that. It was the dead she was wrong about: they can come back.

And not all of them are patient.

Part One ~

The White Lady's Headstone

Padraig O'Doule was a Dowser. Which was good, except when it wasn't.

You see the problem with Paddy—or his dowsing, depending on how you looked at it—was that he tended to find what people hid on purpose, stuff they didn't want found.

Dirty things. Dark things.

And digging up secrets—ugly or otherwise—had a way of getting people angry. And angry people—depending on who they were—were dangerous. Dangerous to Paddy. Dangerous to me, his best mate, Declan Flood.

Dangerous to a whole lot of folk, as it turned out.

But it's not like them mad, malignant folk plant markers saying "Leave this one be, ya daft bastard!"

So I ask you, how could we have known?

It started a fair enough day. The snow was weeks gone. An earnest sun was peeking through the trees, pledging yet another summer. The birds were larking away and the air was all snappy with new green and hawthorn. I was along for the shoveling and Paddy was just doing what he always did, that morning in the woods: dowsing. Which is how we found a locket atop a little hill.

4

I had turned the spade maybe three times before Paddy bent over and plucked it from the dirt.

"Shit me," I said. "That looks old."

"Fookin' yeah it does," Paddy answered. "Worth a bit, you think?"

"Two silver, if it's olden."

Paddy spit, rubbed with his thumb. It gleamed through the smeary mud. "Fookin' flash is what it is, Dec. Two for sure."

"Lemme see," I cried, and he tossed it my way.

Round, heavy, flat as a river stone, it fit nicely in my palm. I hefted it for show, then winked at Paddy before scrutinizing the finding.

Saliva and tobacco juice had cleared the loam to reveal that dull yellow we were so keen on. I hawked my own sauce and rubbed more.

Indeed, indeedy do, gold is what it was. Curious, a precious thing hiding in these workaday woods.

But even curiouser was the engraving; tiny, twisty script coiling around the edge, spiraling in to the center. Or spiraling out from the center, depending on how you looked at it.

I had stayed in school 'til my secondaries, but these weren't like any letters I'd ever seen. "Gold, yes. Olden, maybe. Foreign, sure as sure," I murmured.

"Three silver!" Paddy shouted with a wild, happy grin. "Done for the day, I say. We hit Fade's on the way back to town. Cash up, then it's Teagan's best in my cup for lunch."

"And dinner."

"And dinner," Paddy admitted.

Teagan Cooney ran the local watering hole, and she was good for plenty, including leaving you to sleep at the tables, providing you'd tipped back enough of her cider. She was the easy part of the plan. Fade was another matter.

Meechum Fade was a purveyor of 'Curiosities and Antiques', which mostly meant busted old farm furniture and oddments scrounged from the town dump. A thick boar of a man, he was a notorious skinflint, and the only pawn for twenty miles in any direction.

Local wag had Fade being somebody of mention in his younger days, most popular story painting him a fancy-pants banker who fell afoul of his patron for skimming too much cream off the action. Tale went he barely escaped the garroter, fleeing ireful gentry in the wee hours with naught but the clothes on his back and a purse full of silver crowns. When he finally ran out of steam, he found himself in Carn, County Crae, so he changed his moniker, hung a shingle, and set to fleecing us locals in a vain attempt to regain his fortune. Meechum Fade traded his silks and big head pomp for a life of homespun anonymity with his head still attached.

Whoever Fade used to be, he'd been heaped behind his counter like a sack of unwashed laundry, haggling over knickknacks day in

6

and day out for near ten years. He had a scowly, jowly baby face, two tufts of wire brush hair at odds with his dome, and a jeweler's loupe 'petually screwed in one eye. Grunts and numbers being the extent of his conversations, to say Fade was a tight fist of few words would be generous indeed.

At the very back of Fade's, under a long and battered brass piano lamp, stood a small glass case of assorted shiny bits: ancient pocket watches leashed to tarnished chains, jilted nuptial bands, loops of spindly silver necklaces, Grannie's old brooch...two shelves of mothy velvet lined with memories bartered away for a handful of copper. Paddy was sure ole Fade would nudge a space for this pretty dollop of mislaid bygones, easy as pie. Then the two of us could enjoy the rewards of our labor for a pair of days, at least.

Cupping it like a scoop of water on one hand, I lifted the locket close and traced the swirly script with my other finger. I squinted in case it'd help with ciphering. Paddy leaned in to watch me, the both of us bent over, breathing all nosey and hush-like. But it was no use. Any reading off that spider scratch needed a big city preceptor with a tonsure and halitosis.

Just then, the sky dropped like a wool tarp and the light drained right out of the woods. The air turned with a nip. A bank of clouds had rolled in. My finger must have hit the latch in that same instant, because the face popped up like a cricket.

Paddy jumped back. "Fook, Dec, ya startled me."

A chill bit my thumb where I was holding the rim, but I squeezed out a laugh. "Near widdled my knickers too." I smirked. "Look at us, all scaredy at some skirt's old trinket."

Paddy jutted his chin. "So open it then, you're so plucky."

I teased the lid back with my finger...and there she was. The saddest, prettiest girl I'd ever laid eyes on.

There are plenty of lookers in County Crae, the Sweeney Triplets being at the top of my To Do list. But this one...this girl was near holy as an angel; fancy dress, dark hair bundled up, long neck, fine, high cheeks. A mouth sweet as a plum and made for kisses. She was the kind of woman you go to war in distant lands for, fair as a summer's eve, eternal as the moon.

Loveliness drew your gaze, but it was her loneliness that threw the bolt. Made me want to cry, the sadness seeping off that tiny face. It was like every love ever lost and every promise ever broken, a stain deeper than the sepia she was colored in.

Strangest of all was her eyes were shut.

Not screwed tight in a pique or playing coy, but like the daguerreotype had caught her sleeping, charmed like some princess in a fairy tale. All that beauty frozen still as the grave.

"Fook me, if she ain't the queen of somewhere," Paddy whispered.

All I could do was nod.

Winds kicked up, heavy with the iron scent of a brewing storm. The day went dusky and hunched. I shivered, snapped the face of the locket shut.

8

"Come on," Paddy said. "Let's go."

***

We left the woods and cut across the fields straight for town. Neither of us spoke much. I had slipped the locket in my jacket pocket. It was heavy for such a small thing, tugging down almost like it needed burying again. I actually shifted the shovel on my other shoulder to balance it out. My mind was churning like a mill, ruminating whos and hows and whys. All I got was froth for my trouble.

County Crae had a rugged beauty, but it was too poor, too north, with too many boulders and brambles for the titled to fancy our hills for their halls. And there'd been no tell of reivers or brigands for half a century. Pondering the sleeping maiden's pedigree was like wrestling a sainted mystery.

Paddy might have been brooding the same, but most likely he was arithmetic-ing coins with tankards, adding a good tuck, and maybe a tart for dessert. Vicar Duffy always says mortals can only carry so much; when the Lord gives thither, He has to take yon. Paddy had the Touch, sure as sure, but his idea of history was a fortnight past. Like a duck, things rolled off him. He wasn't the type to perplex over much.

Unlike me, the weather was right definite. A wall of thunderheads had piled up and were scudding our way like a giant, dark castle, rumbleous with lightning. I spied rain curtains looming across the fields, so Paddy and I jogged through the barley and made the crossroad just as the first fat drops pelted down. Fades' establishment was in sight.

Hollering, we bounded through the door and paused under the lintel to drip off a bit and let our eyes adjust.

The place was like a root cellar. Or a badger's den. What I imagine a badger's den to be like, anyway. Low ceilings, dim light, crammed with vaguely felonious articles stored against an impending lean season. It had a distinct blend of smells: old wood, damp soil, and pipe tobacco. An avalanche of chairs was froze in one corner, a buttress of cupboards and canning shelves lined one wall. A thicket of unlit lamps bristled along the other. A dozen clocks told a dozen times. Cairns of books were raised on every flat surface, monumenting the demise of some poor sod's literacy. Some reached to the rafters, their gilded titles glistening like veins of Fool's Gold in granite.

And at the back, past all the various and sundry, in a pool of oily yellow light, sat Meechum Fade.

He barely glanced up when were entered. "Shut it tight," he barked.

Paddy nudged me. Three words was a good sign. Fade was downright hearty today.

Paddy took the lead, navigating through the mess like a dancer across a crowded floor. "You're gonna be keen on this one, Mr. Fade."

I set my shovel down and followed in his wake. "Genuine heirloom, this is."

10

Meechum Fade waved us back, grunting disbelief and consent in the same breath. You have to admire eloquence like that.

There was some debate in town as to whether Fade had feet: no one could remember ever seeing him walk. Resulting from a torturous parenthesis during his alleged pilfering and flight, the footless crowd went so far as to assert Fade weren't on a stool at all, but a fancy privy chair on wheels. That way, they said, he could make mud without stopping his coin fondling. Someone always knew someone who swore they'd seen him rolling about his place after dark, poling the floorboards with his ankle stubbies.

Not that anyone could corroborate that bit of tosh, but it was a captivating controversy once you got a few drinks in you.

Paddy was at the counter grinning like a fool, antsy as a puppy. He could taste his share already. I fished the locket out and pressed it into Fade's outstretched palm careful as a communion wafer.

Fade harrumphed, shifted his bulk and bent over our finding.

The storm was in full swing; lightning flickering, thunder booming like cannon, hoofbeats of gusty rain tearing across the slate roof. Maybe the sky did shiver, maybe I just blinked, but the second Fade spotted the locket, I swore he went still as a field mouse in front of a snake.

He sniffed a heartbeat later. "Could be cleaner, but it's not bad."

"It's gold, right?" I asked.

Fade nodded, staring at it.

11

Paddy practically giggled. "So what's the 'praisal?"

Fade tore his gaze away, the sheeny loupe and bright blue eye glued on me instead. "Where'd ya find this?" A hard question with a light touch.

"What? You think there's more?" Paddy asked. "I felt the place brimming with *something*."

"East. In the woods over the creek," I answered.

Fade's bald head bobbed once.

Paddy leaned over. "Open it," he said helpfully. "Catch is on the edge. The lass innit is pretty as May."

The big man ran a hesitant finger around the rim. Twice. Nothing happened.

"Here," Paddy grabbed for it. "Let Dec try. He did it afore— "

"I believe you," Fade said quickly, and the locket disappeared into the folds of his apron like a magic trick.

"So you'll take it?" Paddy queried.

"Six silver," Fade pronounced.

My mouth dropped open. Paddy yipped with glee.

Two stacks of tarnished copper slid our way. "Three in pennies now. The rest tomorrow."

Paddy's hand swept in like a hawk, scooped up the coins. "Done."

The blue eye fixed me again, the merchant's words soft as sand over gravel. "And you won't be noising this about." Old Fade wasn't requesting; it was a condition of the sale.

"So you do think there's more," Paddy said. "We'll head back—"

"I think you needs keep your cheese pipe shut." Fade bit off each word.

I stared. The dumpy man had turned sharp around the edges. I had a sudden worry how deep it went.

Paddy didn't notice. He was clinking coins one hand into the other like drops off a spigot, already down the road at Teagan's.

"Don't you worry about us, Mr. Fade. We'll be otherwise occupied."

Our audience concluded, Meechum Fade waved us off with a stare that held me responsible.

***

The fire was roaring at Teagan's and so was the crowd. Morning might have pulled everyone out of bed to work but the storm drove them into the pub. Her place was stuffed tighter than Fade's, the debris being entirely the talkative human sort.

Paddy and I shook ourselves like dogs as we entered, raising a volley of groans. We got a cheer in the next breath when Paddy announced we'd come with money to spend.

Ripe and round as a prize-winning pumpkin, sharp and sweet as a Bramley apple, Teagan Cooney was an empress of the bedlam, weaving through the flurry like a shuttle through a racing loom, brace of tankards in one hand, a tray of cups and biscuits in the other. She rolled her eyes when she spotted us. "Plant yerselves where you can. Get to you when I do."

Paddy and I picked our way towards the hearth where the promise of a round was enough for Meany and his farm hands to scoot some room near the fire.

I kicked off my boots and propped 'em on a stack of logs. Water hissed off the leather straight away. I wiggled my stocking toes and fancied peeling my socks off as well, but Teagan's voice rang out behind me.

"Don't you dare, Declan darlin'. You'll owe me lost revenue, clearing the room with them stinky things."

I glanced up. Teagan beamed down. "Now what'll it be?" she asked.

I snuck an arm around her ample waist. "Ach, love. I'm just wringing myself out after a hard day's work and a good drenching." I faked a sneeze. "I could catch my death."

"It's barely noon," she countered. "And the only affliction ever bit you was the blue sky flu."

I clasped my chest in mock injury. "Hard words to wound my heart."

"Truth cuts deep, darlin'."

"But not deeper than Cupid's dart that struck me when first I laid eyes on you."

She blew a stray lock of blonde hair out of her face. "Spare me the pudding. Where's the beef?"

I pinched her quick. "Well, if you put it that way..."

She slapped my hand, then raised one skeptical eyebrow. "It true you pair are flush?"

14

"Indeed, indeedy do, luv, " I assured her.

Paddy jingled his purse. "And there's more coming."

Teagan shook her head. "I'm sure there's a story in that. The good Lord loves fools and drunks."

"Innocent of the first charge, yer Honor," I cried out. "But we'll be working on the second, eh lads?"

Everyone at the table whooped. Meany spoke up from the end stool. "Next round's on them, for certain."

"And the next," Paddy added.

They all passed their cups to Teagan. I pressed five coppers into her hand with a wink. "And keep 'em coming."

She stole a glance at the coins, sniffed in approval, then bustled off.

"And a loaf of bread with butter," I called out. "Please."

She beamed me a smile over her shoulder, tossed her hips ever so sly. Good manners will carry you where money won't, my Ma used to say. I was kinda hoping both would bring me all the way before the day was out.

"And some chicken." Paddy called out.

"Chicken?" Meany asked. "Bit early for supper, don't you think?"

"What?" Paddy blinked. "Bit of leg would be nice right now."

"It would indeed," I snorted.

The whole table roared with laughter.

***

It stopped bucketing sometime late afternoon. I'm fuzzy on the when, the rest of my day going as planned, libation-wise. With half the village present and me with ready coin, there were old debts due and new favors to stow up. Plus, discretion not being the better part of Paddy's valor, I kept veering the chinwag with yet another round every time he strayed too close to specifics. Fade had been dead serious and I wasn't about to test his iron. Thankfully, Paddy being Paddy, he was taken with more salt than oats.

My Da used to say if a man has to be careful not to drink too much, it means he can't be trusted when he does. Well, things in the pub got so rowdy, we near blew off the thatch. But Teagan came out from around the bar a couple times to make sure it all stayed proper.

I recall several bouts of arm wrestling, some dice (win up, lose down, end back at the start. Ain't that the story of my life.). A fierce round of darts 'tween Meany's crew and the blacksmith's boys, one fight betwixt the same, followed by ardent apologies and a couple ditties with verses I can't repeat in polite company. By the time the crowd had staggered home, my purse was far lighter than I wanted. But it was worth every cent.

Even better, I had the promise of more tomorrow, so I'd call that a good day.

When my head finally stopped swimming, the fire was fairy flames dancing on a bed of embers. Night had inked in the windowpanes solid raven. The pub was empty save me and Paddy, me well snattered and him snoring in the corner.

I licked my lips and looked down. My socks were dry and still on my feet, as opposed to in my mouth like it tasted. I nicked a heel of bread from the ruins of somebody's dinner and was gnawing away when Teagan plopped down beside me.

"Cup of tea with that?" she piped up.

I bit back a groan. "Right nice of you to ask."

A steaming mug appeared on the table in front of me.

I sipped and scalded the roof of my mouth. It didn't matter. "Have I told you I love you?" I croaked.

"A thousand times."

"I meant every word." I ogled her bosom. "Some parts more than others perhaps."

She punched me on the shoulder, tugged up her blouse.

"Easy, love, I'm all delicate," I cried. I composed what I hoped was a serious face. "So when are you going to marry me, Tea?"

"What, and leave all this?" She spread her hands and gestured around the room.

"To feed, trough and muck out a herd of fluthered men?"

"It's in my blood; four generations of dealing with the besotted."

"I'm being earnest here," I said.

"So am I." She laughed. "You're asking me to feed, trough and muck up after you, only with a baby on each hip. No, thank you."

I put on a sulk, threw the crust into the fire.

"Quit your pouting, Declan darlin'. You're in need of a good sleep, not a good snoggin'."

"I get to choose?"

She peeled off a frown and changed the subject. Case closed. Teagan leaned over and nodded at Paddy. "So...what'd he dowse up?"

I shrugged, grumpy. Hoping against hope for a repeal. Got me a stern look instead.

"Guess I'll be tallying your bar tab now," she said idly.

Teagan Cooney could be as hard as nails when she wanted. One more reason I was so keen on her.

"Bit of jewelry. Gold." I finally answered.

She whistled. "Olden?"

"Dunno," I shrugged. "Foreign, more like. A piece with gravened letters like I'd never seen." That tiny face leapt to mind and I wondered at all that lovely sadness. "It was nice though."

Teagan poked my ribs. "How nice?"

"Six crowns nice."

She squeaked. "Fade forked over *six* for it? Practically a sign of the second coming, that is. Silver out of him is like pulling teeth." She stared at the blushing coals for a long minute. "Must be worth a heap if he's willing to part with that much. There more?"

I waved at Paddy, who was snoozing away with a faint smile on his lips. "Could be. Felt *something* big, he said."

"Treasure in County Crae..."she mused. "Where?"

"Pick and spade at the crack of dawn? That your plan?" I asked.

She shook her head and laughed pretty as a flute. "Finders keepers, Dec. Seems like there's plenty to go 'round anyway."

"East in the woods. Past the creek on a little hill."

"Near a copse of rowans?"

"And how do you know that?" I demanded.

"*Cloch chinn d'ailbe bhean,*" she said, and crossed herself.

"Come again?"

There was something of a fright in her eyes when she looked up. "The White Lady's Headstone. That's what my Ma called the place."

A log snapped. We both started. Not especially religious, I had the urge to cross myself all of a sudden, too.

Still, fear might have its uses, but cowardice never did. I turned to face Teagan. "Do tell," I said.

"She was little," Teagan began. "We're talking donkey's years, before the Fichti mounted Prince Aedh's head on a pike, when Airam was still the second in line—the 'heir and the spare' so to speak."

"Handy, having an extra," I muttered.

"Lucky for King Arnaw they did. Anyways, my Gran had sent her for mushrooms or to turn up some lost sheep. I can't remember which. She told me she'd been traipsing around the other side of the creek all afternoon, and dark was coming fast."

Another sip of tea. "Not that this ain't fascinating, love..."

19

She scowled. "That morning a royal coach had passed though Carn, she said. All gilt and paint, drawn by big fine horses."

"Royal? Says who?"

"She said there was fancy banners, pages with horns, and a detachment of guards decked out in polished armor. It didn't stop. Ma said they all figured it was heading to Daire on the coast. Lord knows why it was coming through Carn, but no one durst ask. A quick kneel, then back to chores. No one gave it any mind after."

Teagan continued. "Ma remembers the rowan fruit was in full bloom, big clusters hanging off the branches like fat blood marbles. It was supper time, and she was eating a handful when she spied 'em."

"Who, the guards?"

"The whole kit and boodle, carriage and all. Only it was parked near the little hill and there was two ladies standing outside it carrying on."

"Two ladies? Gentry?"

"Aye. Flouncy dresses, bangles, faces sharp as hawks. One young and pretty, the other handsome, but old enough to be her ma."

"Having a row in the woods? She heard 'em?"

"Not exact but enough to get the meaning. Ma said it was all shrieks and nails. She remembers Prince Airam's name came up several times. And the King."

I motioned for Teagan to continue.

"Ma said the arguing crested, then the older one looked past the younger to a big soldier standing by and made this little motion with her hand. Then she turned her back on the girl."

"The lass get mad?"

"Probably, but Ma said the instant the lady turned away, this big soldier stepped up behind the girl quiet as a shadow and cut her throat.

"He what?"

Teagan nodded solemnly. "In one stroke. Like she was a lamb. Ma said blood sheeted down the front of the fancy dress like a waterfall, snow white turning red as roses. The older lady kept looking away, still as a statue."

"Then what?"

"She ran."

"Who?"

She hit me with the towel again. "My ma, you twit. Who'dja think?" Teagan paused. "Never ate another rowan berry to this day."

I absorbed that, thought another minute. "She tell anyone?" I finally asked.

"Obvious she told me, innit?"

"Right. I mean back then."

Teagan shook her head slowly. "Locked it up inside for years. Not even a peep in the confessional. She really gonna spill to the Vicar? Or slog all the way to Daire or Dubhlinn for a magister? Her word 'gainst a royal lady...they'd have cut her tongue out."

I chewed my lip, remembering that girl's sleeping grief. Getting your neck opened would be tragic, sure as sure. "Your Ma remember seeing any jewelry? Like a big locket 'round one of their necks?"

"I told you it was too far for particulars."

An idea crashed into me: Fade hadn't paid in full yet, so I could borrow the locket back first thing tomorrow. Just long enough to trudge over to Ma Conney's for part of the day. "You think she'd recognize the lass if she saw a picture?"

"Get the wax out, Dec. What'd I just say?"

Teagan was right that I wasn't listening. That tiny face had a hook in me, and I had a strange notion it would ease her sorrow if I solved the riddle. Somehow.

I was teetering on explaining when Paddy snorted awake.

He belched, rubbed his face. "Hullo." Freckles, hair mushed up on one side, he looked like a kid up from a nap.

Teagan passed him the rest of my tea. "Here. More's coming." She gave me a 'hush, now' look, and went back to the kitchen.

I watched Paddy blink himself awake, and my heart swelled. Simple as he could be at times, there wasn't a drop of spoil in him.

We'd been born in the same month, and with our parents' farms

separated by a single stone wall, we'd been best mates since we were in nappies. My Da had drilled into me to never desert a friend. So even after it came out Paddy was touched, I stuck by him. In the fields, in town, at school, wherever, all growing up. Twenty-three years, I never got him into any trouble I couldn't get him out of. And after the fever took my parents—God rest their souls—he was all the family I had left in this world. But dead girls, old jewelry, murderous royalty... I was out of my depth here.

22

Teagan was right; too much drink and drama, not enough sleep. My head would be screwed on better in the morning. After a good breakfast—and the other half of my share from Fade. That made me smile.

I stood, floorboards creaking and swaying under my feet. "Paddy," I said, "where are my boots?"

He looked at me bleary, a curious grin on his face.

I lifted one stocking foot above the table height. "They were drying this morning. And now...?"

Paddy focused a moment, staring off into some middle distance I'd never see. I felt the hair on the back of my neck stand. "One's under that table," he pointed. "The other's outside."

"Outside? How the—?"

He cocked his head at me as if I should know."By the outhouse."

Took me a quarter hour hopping around the yard with a lantern, but I found it. Teagan thought it was hilarious.

***

Paddy and I aimed our way toward our rooms at Widow Halloran's. Carn was sound asleep all around us and we meandered down the street between wagon ruts, trying to remember the more behaved verses of a tune about a ship named Venus. Thankfully, it was near bright as noon. The storm had scoured the sky clean, leaving a huge buttermilk moon adrift in a dark sea of stars. A stiff breeze

23

ferried the sharp balm of pine and damp earth over fields brimming with cricket song. It was a beautiful evening after a near perfect day.

"You're sweet on Teagan," Paddy said, out of the blue.

Teagan had this husky chuckle that made me go all warm, and I'd been thinking on her when he spoke. "Touch tell you that?" I snapped.

He looked at me, hurt. "Plain as day, Dec. Everybody knows it. Not just me."

I felt bad, shooting my mouth off. "Sorry," I mumbled. "Sore subject."

He smiled brightly. "You're in luck. She's sweet on you."

"Everybody know that too?" I sputtered.

"Nope." He shook his head. "But she is. I can tell."

I thought of the cold bed I was heading to. "Sure has a funny way of showing it."

Paddy held onto his words for a moment like he wondered if he should let them out. "I get the notion she's waiting on you to grow up a little," he finally said.

"Away with that!" I stamped my foot. "I'm more than man enough to please her. I'm two years older, easy."

"I mean like 'taking on a steady trade' man enough," Paddy explained. "Don't think she cares exact which. It's ballast she's concerned with. To know you can keep an even keel."

That ruffled my feathers even more. Family land was sold when my parents died, and I couldn't see myself steaming slats at the cooperage or heaving bellows for the town smith. Same as Paddy didn't dwell on the past, I'd stopped giving mind to the future several years back.

Still, hope flickered in me. "You're on the level?" I asked.

"Sure as sure."

I confess my heart skipped. I promised myself I'd call on her the next day, after Fade paid up. Have a sit-down and little chat. In that moment, the future seemed something worth considering.

Paddy and I was at the edge of town, working on a new verse for the boat song, when we saw Fade's place.

It was lit up bright as a Christmas hooley, windows blazing like every lamp the fat man owned was at full wick.

"Fade's working late," I smirked. "Must be milkin' nickels for extra pennies." The dark shape of a figure moved inside. I started for the door. "Bet he's got our other half now."

I turned to grin at Paddy and found him rooted in place, middle of the road, tears streaming down his cheeks. He was staring at Fade's.

My hackles rose. I started to speak. "What's the ma—?"

Then a scream, wild, deep and gurgly. Like a horse being slaughtered.

It came from inside.

Fear sobered me faster than a bucket of ice. I spun around and peered at the shop windows. The moving inside had stopped.

I'd be lying if I didn't say part of me wanted to run like smoke and oakum. The stubborn part of me won out though. Blame curiosity, blame greed. Teagan says it was destiny.

I crept toward the door.

I struck new deals with myself every step. I'll knock twice, I said. If he answers, then all is well. If he's ready with our money now, fine. If not, tomorrow will come soon enough. If it's locked, I'll be on my merry. I'll knock once...

I rapped a knuckle on the oak. The door creaked open an inch. Unlocked, unlatched.

Shite, shite, shite, shite...

I pushed the door further. "Mr. Fade?"

Silence.

"Evening, Mr. Fade. You in here?" Save a pair of lanterns in the back, the room was dark. No sign of a fire, candles, nothing. The bright light had been snuffed like a match.

I tiptoed over the threshold, goose-fleshed head to toe. "It's me, Declan Flood."

I grabbed a coal poke from a bin of rusty tools and gripped it two-handed like a club. Nothing appeared out of sorts from that morning, but the air was thick with jitters. I felt someone else's footsteps, the sense I'd catch 'em slinking into the shadows out of the corner of my eye.

The back of my neck tingled with spiders but I took another step. "Alrighty then," I yelled. "Whoever's in here come out now or I'll brain you to next Sunday." Bravest words I could conjure.

26

Fade was in his usual spot, slumped back, mouth open wide. I listened for a snore I half knew wasn't coming.

If it was thieves, were they still about? Crouched behind the counter, waiting to spring up and throttle me? "Stop your sneaking, whoever you are. I'm armed and you're getting me downright wrathful."

Coal poke cocked, I crept around the end and rounded on the old man's seat. His coins were stacked in neat little ranks like soldiers. The glass curio case was undisturbed. I hoped to hear Fade's breathing, but all I got was the thrum of my own heart hammering in my ears.

Meechum Fade was deader than a bag of rocks.

Against my smarter half, I dared a look at his face. Terror is what it read.

Mouth open, wide-eyed, bowel-clenching terror. Like Fade had glimpsed Old Nick himself. It froze my blood.

Right then, Paddy's voice rang out behind me. "Look!"

I spun and swung, missing him by a hair.

"Jesus Almighty!" I shouted. "Near jumped out of my skin, you twit!" I was all prickly fear there'd be a grinning skull or some toady demon, squatting in the corner all venomous and malefic.

He ignored me, pointing down. "He's got feet!"

"Fook me, " I sighed, and set the coal poke down.

After my heart stopped racing, Paddy leaned toward Fade.

"Funny—"

"No, it wasn't." I said. "Pranking around the dead must be some brand of blasphemy."

Paddy wasn't listening. "He opened the locket."

Indeed, Meechum Fade was clutching the locket— *our* locket. And the lid was up, the strange script coiling like a snake.

I lifted it quiet as a whisper out of Fade's meaty palm and peered down at that face yet again.

She was as lovely as I remembered; dark hair, full mouth, face like a sleeping angel. But something had changed.

She was smiling.

Part Two ~

Beneath the Rowan Trees

I heard her in the wee hours.

Faint it was, a lament tattered in the wind. A lost bird crying for summer.

A name.

She was weeping over a name.

I creaked down the stairs one at a time and stepped out into the yard.

The moon had dropped in the west. It was deep night; those dark hours when only dreams and the eyes of God roam the earth. The sky was salted with stars, winking vast and distant, drawing everything around me in black shapes and stiff shadows.

The wind caressed my face, wet and warm after the storm, like a horse's breath. Heavy and familiar. I smelled grass in the meadow, the clean snap of the river, earthy loam from the woods where she called.

The moon peeked through a scrap of low clouds, so I set out east across the silver rippled fields, toward the heavy green budding over trunks straight and tall as a thicket of spears, to the woods where we found the locket. To that voice.

Seemed like no time I parted the brush, plunged in. The rustle of leaves underfoot.

Her voice was louder. Drawing me onward.

I didn't remember the creek but suddenly my feet were wet. I considered kicking my boots off to dry like at Teagans... and there she was: a pale moth flitting in the timber. A dark haired beauty in a white dress, weeping as she hurried deeper into the woods.

I heard the name clear: Airam. The king's name.

"Airam, my only, my love, my prince. Where are you?"

She stops among the trees. Her back to me, raven tresses tumbling, hands clenched in pretty little knots at her side... She tilts her head back and forth as she searches, but doesn't look my way because I'm not the one she seeks, her love, her only.

No one is there to comfort her, and her voice breaks with heartache. I want to be that one. To see those eyes open, have them to look for me. To fall into them...

She runs. Runs toward that little hill.

I'm after her. Branches snapping, whipping my face and arms. I'm bleeding from a dozen scratches but I don't care; she's crying again and every tear is a blow to my chest. My heart cracks.

Anything to ease her pain, dry those tears. "I'm here," I want to say. "I'll be your only, your love."

She runs on, but I'm faster. Every step a step closer.

Suddenly she's in a copse of trees, sobbing in a pool of moonlight. Her shoulders shudder like the sorrow of the world is pouring out of her. Out of her, into my bones, under my skin, into my heart... I'm in her agony, looking through tears to God, to the vast and

31

distant stars, the bile of her loss on my tongue, and I see now... see now we're under the rowan trees.

The branches bow with fruit, clusters of plump blood silver hanging like a Judas-kiss, shivering me like a death sentence.

She calls out again. "Airam? My love. Where are you?"

Her voice yanks me back. I reach out to her quaking shoulders, words on my lips. "There, there. I'll help you."

My hand grazes white ruffle. She spins, bristling like a cat.

I jump back.

It's all wrong; that loveliness has curdled. Her hair is crazed, her face fever-twisted, rancid with grief. There's a drench of red glistening stickily down the front of her damask silk. She's grinning like a dead hare, teeth bared over a neck gaping like a second mouth. Her hands snatch at me, claws to pull me in.

I scuttle back, but she pursues. I stumble. Her eyes snap open: two seething blanks, blistering white coals of desolation and rage. I am ruined.

"Where. Is. My. LOVE?" She shrieks the final word, neck and mouth in hideous concert.

The sound guts me like a spear— keening from the chasm of hell. The wailing damned on the Day of Judgment. My heart seizes up.

It's a scream to wake the dead.

Or kill the living.

She lunges for me.

***

I flail in my bed like a drowning man and bolt upright.

Moonlight is spilling through the window onto the floor. The cupboard is a humped shadow in the corner. The house is quiet save Paddy's soft snoring next door.

My heart starts again and I'm alone in my room with that scream ringing in my ears.

***

We took back the locket, Paddy and me, on account of Fade being dead and us being the original finders of merchandise not paid in full. We could have completed the transaction—the coins stacked on his counting board all neat and shiny—but Vicar Duffy assures us there's a special place in hell for pilfering stiffs. Even though Fade was barely cold, that sat a shade too near grave-robbing for my liking.

So on the spot, Paddy and me branded our prior deal with the fat man a temporary exchange, like a loan, and I swore him to secrecy. "We're fair and square now, so not a word to another soul," I explained.

Paddy nodded at my logic, spat solemnly, and we shook on it. After all, we'd gotten the better end of the deal. Why poke at it further?

While Paddy ran to wake Mayor Tom and old Angus, the shire-reeve, I slipped the locket back into my jacket.

Truth was, I had the strangest notion I shouldn't leave it, that I couldn't abandon *her* to the callow eye of some sour-faced magistrate or the light-fingered clerks who'd be divvying the dead man's earthly goods.

It was in my cupboard now, wrapped in a sock under my second best pair of pants. Which after the dream, was uncomfortable close.

Maybe I expected it to start thumping like a rabbit in a box, or for her to step out into my room, neck and all, coming for me with those hands and smoldering eyes. Whatever the case, sleep was done with me for the night.

I sat in my bed peering at that sideboard 'til dawn crept through the dormers.

***

Because Meechum Fade had been a landowner, his passing needed to be scribed at the county seat, at Daire on the coast. The mayor sent Willem, his eldest, on horseback to notify whoever needed knowing. Fade had no relations that any knew of, certainly none in County Crae, so no family meant no wake, and no wake meant there'd be a no big feed for weeping friends and reminiscing neighbors.

Truth be told, near ten years in Carn, not a single soul could say they knew the fat man more'n "How do you do." I thought it a shame on both accounts, although I'd wager those in arrearage breathed a sigh of relief.

The grieving have a saying about observances for the dearly departed: "High money, high mass. Low money, low mass. No money, no mass." Now, I'm near certain Fade never dropped so much as a bent penny in the plate, but Vicar Duffy announced he'd hold a noon vigil for anyone interested in greasing the big man's passage to

34

Abraham's Bosom. He even let them dig a hole in the corner yard on church ground. The liturgy and burying were slated for afternoon the following day. Best get the dead on their way, Vicar Duffy says. No sense lingering over an empty sack.

He was one of the better ones, Duffy was. Short, stout, and ugly as a bulldog chewing a wasp, he hid a heart of gold behind a sharp mind and a sharper tongue. For the longest time, I thought all clerics were like him: part mean, part mad, part saint, part sad. Wasn't 'til I was older I learned how lucky Carn was to have him standing in for the Lord.

After breakfast, Mayor Tom and Angus put me and Paddy through the wringer over the particulars of the previous evening. The dream had me stretched thin, but we stuck to the plan; the locket was ours. Those two fired a baker's dozen of the same questions over and over 'til we all were near tearing our hair out. Paddy stayed the course and I was right proud of him.

Not that we were slinging smoke and shite; we saw lights, heard a yelp, barged in to render a hand. We just kept mum about the locket.

The church bell was ringing when they finally let us go. "Apologies for the grilling, but we need our ducks in a row for this 'un," Mayor Tom pronounced. "Shame you lads had to find him freshly croaked. I'm proud you manned up and fetched us straight away."

"Better'n later, after the body's turned," Angus grumbled. "Try corpse-duty after a battle. That'll tickle your nose hairs. Stench sticks on ya three days. Why, one time when I was in the regiment—"

"Sobering thing it is, being reminded of your mortality," the Mayor said quickly. "Sounds like the Vicar's starting the service. I think we'd better let these lads get to prayers." He winked and shooed us out the door.

Angus O' Hagan had chased Fichti raiders with the King's Own back when he had hair and younger knees. He claimed his limp resulted from a close call with a war axe, and after a swallow or three, was forever ready with the blow by blow of the famous incident. His wife blamed gout and was always after him to drop a few stone.

Paddy and I ducked out the door faster than scalded dogs. "Don't be running off either," Angus called out. "In case we got more questions."

"Where does he think we're going to go?" Paddy asked when we were down the street a pace. "This is the only home we got."

We were walking up the church steps when I decided that was the smartest query I'd heard all morning.

***

Noon Mass was exciting as watching paint dry; all mumbles, chants and candles. Still, a fair number of town folk came to click the beads for Meechum Fade. Perhaps some were thanking the Almighty for writing off their earthly outstandings and figured they'd do Fade a turn with his spiritual ones. All I know for certain is the Good Lord and his Vicar had mercy on us and kept it to an hour.

36

Afterwards though, when Paddy went chatting after Fiona Sweeney out into the yard, I lingered in the nave. The dream had frayed me good and I needed gathering.

The chapel was warm from the bodies, musky with incense and beeswax smoke. The colored glass windows glowed in the afternoon sun bright as iron straight from a forge. Hewn beams stretched through the dark ceiling like tree limbs, which set me thinking on her.

To be honest, I never felt much sacredness during holy services. I know the catechism declares church to be hallowed ground, God's outpost where heaven touches earth, but filled with people, it's more a barn dance... only boring, in Latin, and with no dancing. Most folks don't thank God and mean it until the Vicar says the last "Amen".

Being alone in church was a whole other kettle of fish.

Soul's truth was if I went still for a minute, let the quiet settle over me, I felt watched. A penetrating kind of seeing, but not harsh. More like someone who knew me waiting on my next move.

In that moment, I confess I hadn't a clue to what that was. The locket, Teagan's story, Fade's death, the smile ... yesterday swirled in my head madder than a swarm of bees. I was as forlorn as my murdered dream girl wandering the moon-shadowed trees, weeping for a lost lover.

I was near lighting a taper to St. Anthony to help me find my right mind when Vicar Duffy sidled up beside me. Second time in less than a day I near jumped out of my skin. "Shame it takes the dead to get you through these doors nowadays," he said.

Took two breaths before I could give the Vicar a sheepish grin. "Figured I'd do right by the man, being one of the last to see him."

He fixed me with a pointed look. "How'd that go, that last time you saw Meechum?"

A sudden bead of sweat tickled my neck. I joked it off. "Well enough on my part. Seeing as I was still breathing."

Vicar Duffy nodded, looked toward the altar. "My heart's been worried for you lately, Declan. You and Paddy." He turned back to me. "Any idea why?"

That watched feeling dropped on my shoulders solid as two bales of hay, the urge to spill sitting even heavier.... but that would mean I'd have to own up to the locket, to nicking it back from a dead man, to the dream, the smile. Thieving *and* mad as a hatter—that wouldn't do. Muck of it would be on Paddy too.

No.

I managed to shake my head.

Vicar Duffy held my gaze half a second, then looked back to the altar. "Well then, I'll keep praying God's mercy on you."

We stood there, candles guttering, happy noises trickling in from the yard. The watching got heavier.

Finally. "Vicar," I said. "I know the creeds, the Holy Writ, but..." I fumbled for the words. "Have you ever been... smacked by something that rattled you, threw everything you thought on its head?"

That was the best I could do.

Vicar Duffy didn't blink. "Of course, Declan. That's why I keep praying."

"Well then, I could use a bit of wisdom, too," I said after a moment.

He looked at me curiously.

"No offense," I added quickly. "I mean so long as you're asking."

Vicar Duffy laughed and clapped me on the shoulder. "Okay, then. I'll add wisdom to the list."

We started toward the doors.

"When are you going to marry Teagan Cooney?" he asked.

"She's a fine girl."

"Jesus Almighty!" I cried, then blushed. "Sorry Vicar." I shuffled a bit. "The whole town know?"

He nodded, holding back a huge grin.

Flustered, I took off down the stairs and made a beeline for Paddy. "I'm working on it," I called over my shoulder.

"I'll add that as well," he shot back. "Just don't belabor it too long."

***

Next day, I was stunned to see most of County Crae at the funeral. Word had spread. Guess if a decade planted in the same soil didn't render a man friendly, it at least made him a fixture. Even if Fade's memoriam was more like a tip of the hat to an old mill than actual mourning, the little stone church was crammed.

The local notables were all preened and proper, present on the front row. Three generations crowded the pews all the way to the back wall, and I saw field hands kneeling on the steps. Dressed in our best, Paddy and I used our elbows and notoriety to carve out a good spot on the porch.

The Vicar droned the usual "ashes to ashes" over a largish pine box, praying mercy on a soul that had been disinclined to either charity or cheer. Mercy being just that, I joined in the asking, especially on account of the locket stashed in my cupboard.

Stranger still, the eulogy cleared a bit of fog surrounding Meechum's history. Turned out he'd been a soldier in his early days, trading blows with the Norse, the Fichti, even the Franks. The big man ended up a sergeant at arms in the Royal Guard, in fact, and had been discharged with honors by Her Majesty, Queen Niamh. God only knew why Fade picked Carn to settle in, but he did. Of course this was a while back, before dotage and fever ushered King Arnaw into a marble sepulcher. The years had certainly padded Fade out a bit, but the steel in his voice the other night suddenly made sense. Funny, the things you never suspect in a man 'til it's too late.

Niamh was Queen Mother now, perched in a fancy hall on the cliffs overlooking the harbor outside Daire. Her youngest son wielded the Emerald scepter these days, King Airam.

Revelations continued after the service; indeed, it was a loaves and fishes miracle that anything at all happened after the burying. As soon as the first shovelfuls hit the lid, the Mayor popped up and invited everyone to Teagan's for a repast "In honor of a hero of the realm and pillar in the community." A whoop and holler went round.

Seemed Meechum Fade was set on leaving a good impression. Looking back, if I'd had a lick of sense, I'd have asked myself who was footing the bill, but never ones to pass on free food and drink, Paddy and I angled for Teagan's straightaway.

My Da used to say, "Before, you're smart; after, you're wise. In between you're otherwise." Tough old bastard was right. I just hope I grab myself by the scruff of the neck before I jump hip-deep into another royal midden.

***

Teagan's place was even louder and more stuffed than the previous day. Poor lass must have been slaving over the coals since I last seen her, the heaps of food weighing down the tables. It was like Christmas and Harvest feast combined.

I was well into my second ale when I spotted the stranger.

41

I didn't like him straight off. Wiry, dark, with a sharp beard and an oily sneer, he was standing with the Mayor and Angus, tankard in hand, sizing up the locals like a shepherd looks for mutton. The cut of his cloth was a giveaway, but all the bobbing and scraping made it plain he was someone of mention.

I was reaching for a plate when Mayor Tom pointed me out to him. The stranger fixed me from across the room, eyes squinched as if he'd just nocked an arrow.

Paddy chose that moment to clap me on the shoulder. "Almost wish Fade had kicked the bucket sooner," he said with his mouth full. "Quite the to-do."

I answered without turning. "What do you make of that posh gouger in the corner?"

Paddy swiveled his head like a goose. "Where?"

"Jesus wept. Don't gawk," I hissed. "With Mayor Tom. He's staring at me."

"Why?"

"If I knew, I wouldn't be asking," I said. "You didn't spill, did you?"

"No," Paddy answered. "You said not to."

I stared at my plate, feeling bad for doubting him. "So?" I asked.

Paddy looked at me, curious. "So...?"

"So why's the hardchaw here? I've never seen him in my life."

"You mean the man with the ferret-face and the fur trim cloak?"

42

"Aye," I sighed.

"Oh, he's looking for someone," he said as if it were the most obvious thing in all creation.

"Who?"

"You."

Gooseflesh burred up and down my arms. I looked up sharply, right as Mayor Tom waved me over. The stranger had disappeared. I threw a quick look over my shoulder.

Shite on a stick.

I threaded my way through the crowd. The Mayor drew me in, cleared his throat all official-like. "Man in town today name of Odhran Kane, captain of the Queen Mother's Guard. He's come all the way from Daire to pay his respects to Fade."

"Served with him guarding Her Majesty," Angus interjected. "Reward for proper soldiering, that is. I could tell Meechum was a hard man. Knew it the minute I laid eyes on him. It's the—"

Mayor Tom waved the older man to silence, looked me square in the eye. "Ain't exactly the mournful type, this Kane. Truth, he's been hard with questions since he swung off his horse."

"Questions?"

"Vicar told him was Fade's heart gave out, but he's exacting chapter and verse on his death, his state, personal effects and the like."

"Royal family paid for this spread," Angus pronounced. "They remember good service. Duty, loyalty, those are—"

43

Mayor Tom pulled me out of earshot. I waited. He weighed his words, then continued. "Listen to me, lad. Kane demanded a word with you in the civic house."

"When?"

"Now."

"Why me? I told you me and Paddy were—"

"I know. I gave him your accounting but he's not one can be denied. Not by me at least."

"What's he after then?"

Worry etched the Mayor's face. "I don't know, Declan, but don't trifle with him, you hear me? Odhran Kane is ill-set, dripping scorn like a leaky barrel. He was practically slavering to put the screws to Paddy, but I shied him off, insisting you were smart as paint and knew your place." He looked me in the eye. "Keep your head. And by all the saints, stick with what you told me. Unnerstand?"

Mayor Tom nudged me toward the door before I could answer.

I made sure Paddy was looking the other way before I ducked out. The Mayor was right; Paddy wouldn't last a second with a hard case like Kane. I'd promised myself and his folks I'd look after him. This was my to-do, not his. I slipped through the crowd and headed toward the center of town, dread gnawing at my bowels.

Carn's civic house had been sired on an ancient mead hall, a veritable fortress from olden times, most likely raised for the first lord of these parts. Refit and gussied up over the years, the main oak and granite walls stood in my mind as staunch and hale as the Twelve

44

Bens, the snow-streaked peaks that guarded every sunrise. Kane's rancor and the heft of them looming stones had it suddenly dungeon-like, more with every step.

Even the man's horse was cross. Wearing tooled leather with silver jangles, a big black stallion was tied at the main door like a sentry. It flat-eared at my approach, then lunged at my shoulder, flaring teeth and nostrils.

"Fook you, ya manky thing. Remind me to poison your apples."

That there was what the Vicar would call a sign. I should have turned around right then. But never one to do things easy, the stubborn part slipped the rest of me past the post and on inside where I searched out Odhran Kane.

A smart old dead fella once said, "The nail that sticks up too high is the first to get hammered." I figure the best way to deal with my betters is to leave 'em thinking they are, lest they start pissing from their high horses. Now I've met precious few men who actually deserved a bow, but a trembly feeling had me bobbing my head the second I crossed the threshold.

Odhran Kane was planted at a table piled with ledgers, the fingers of one hand tracing lines across a wide page. The room stank of musty paper, cologne, and contempt. I knocked, tugged my forelock.

He didn't look up. "I'd have you swinging from the nearest tree."

"Beg your pardon?" I gulped.

The silence hung in the air while he continued tracing columns in the register. Finally he sniffed, stared at me. "For robbery. You admit you were the last to see him, you and your idiot friend."

"Ummm..."

"Money like Meechum's is a powerful incentive." He looked around the room. "Especially in this pig trough."

"I'm sorry, your honor. I don't take—"

He slammed the book and stood to his feet. "Oh you *took* something. You shit-kicking culchies always do. Question is what. Money? Rubbish from that case? Tell me now and I'll leave the imbecile O'Doule be."

"Sir," I started, "we heard 'im yell, barged in ta help. Door was already open, I swear on it—"

Odhran Kane opened the ledger up, flipped through pages until his gloved finger stabbed down. "Flood and O'Doule," he read. "Six Crowns." His gaze glittered like a cat's in candlelight. "Tell me Flood, what's worth *six silver* in a shithole like Carn, hmmmm?"

My heart turned to stone.

He knows. He knows about the locket.

"Sir, me and Paddy—"

"Your half-wit cousin?"

"Yes, sir. I mean, no. He's not my cousin. We was born in the same month—"

Kane snarled, waved me on.

46

"The two of us go digging around the olden places, ruins and such," I stammered. "Sometimes we turn up trinkets Mr. Fade would buy. We found—"

"Meechum Fade was a lot of things. Stupid wasn't one of them," Kane snapped. "Certainly not one to throw hard silver after a bumpkin's rummage and scrap."

My thoughts were boiling furious. Desperation being the mother of invention, I conjured a lie from bits of truth. "It were a sack full. All olden, I think. Mr. Fade were pleased and promised us six silver."

A notion popped in to my head. "But we only got half," I whined. "He promised the rest later, and now he's..."

A smirk twitched across Kane's lips. "And where did you dig up this *treasure*, Flood?"

I scrabbled for an answer. North of town lay the "Teats", half-a-dozen ancient barrows humped under sweet clover and wildflowers. They'd been combed through decades before I came along, but I doubted Odhran Kane knew that. "The olden mounds north of here, sir. We dug all day in the sun. And to only get half isn't fair—"

"Quit mewling or I'll feed your tongue to the pigs," Kane sighed, casually brutal. He rested a hand on a stack of registers. "A sack full, you say?"

I nodded, eyes down.

"Then Fade would have inventoried this hoard, eh? Or if not in the books then I'll find it wrapped in burlap in his shop. Right, Flood?"

47

I nodded again, miserable.

"You're lying," Kane whispered. "I can feel it."

He came around the table, huffing menace with breath that reeked like catshit and gin. "I'll find out the What. Then I'll find out the Why. Then I'll drag you off in irons, cut off your hands, your feet, *your stones*, before I string you up at Daire's Gate for robbery. And murder. You and your dim, inbred cousin. You hear me, Flood?"

I gulped, managed a nod.

"Now get out of my sight."

I ran.

Past the surly horse, past Teagan's place a-bustle with a dead man's party, all the way to the crossroads where Fade's shop sat bolted and shuttered. Going by, it frightened me how life can rush from heaven to hell in a sliver of time. Teagan says it's never the changes we want that change everything. She was right.

I took the stairs at Widow Halloran's two at a time, thinking all I had to do was put it back. Climb in a window, squeeze through the coal chute... hell, shimmy down the chimney if needed. I'd tuck it on a shelf under his counter. Or wrap it in a scrap of linen and stick it in a drawer. I'd confess to it once Odhran Kane found it. I'd beg off my lie on the want of the rest of the money Fade had owed. A smack and a whipping would be the worst of it. So long as it weren't gelding and the noose.

And Paddy would be out of it.

I burst in my room, flung open the cupboard and pawed through my clothes 'til I clutched my woolen sock.

48

It was empty.

The locket was gone.

Part Three -
Lurking and Larceny

It must have been Paddy. And I wasn't sick on the notion he had the locket; more the locket had him. Gold brings one sort of trouble. A screaming dream lass is a whole different matter.

Back at Teagan's, Widow Halloran scoffed like I'd sprouted another head and was still talking out my arse.

"Like I'd sort your dirty linen..." she shouted over the noise of the party." Why don't you ask Teagan, you need someone to scrub your nethers?" She covered a grin with her tankard. "Once a week to change the sheets, I told you that when you started. You and Paddy."

"Have you seen him, then?"

"Who?"

"Paddy?"

"He's 'ere, isn't he?" She glared about the room like he was a middle-grader ducking lessons. A familiar sight, her being the headmistress most of her life.

"Everyone is," she declared. "Look for the Sweeney girls." She turned back to the table, swaying as she did.

At sixty plus years, and slight as a rake, Widow H. could drink most men in town under the table. I'd never met a woman with such a throat on her. Rabbity though I was, I considered the imbibing needed to make her bend in the breeze. Enough to float a raft, I figured.

"If you see him—"

She waved me off. "He'll know you're after him."

Widow Halloran was right: anyone who hadn't been at the funeral was in the tavern now. Teagan's was inside out, festivities spilling into the yards. I spied three competing fiddlers, a throng of dancers, the regular arm-wrestling set, and an even rowdier queue for a brace of tapped barrels. A peck of women had the outdoor hearth blazing, ladling stew and biscuits to all comers. Fade's memorial had converted to a hooley worth gloating on for years to come.

Mindful of Kane's earlier appraisal of County Crae, I wondered at so much ready gold for a dead soldier ten years out to pasture.

Was it to make memories? Or hide them?

The notion it all weaved together chewed at me: Fade, Teagan's story, my dream, Kane... And now Paddy missing with the locket.

At first, I feared Kane changed his tune and hauled him in, but the snakey bastard reappeared at the head table soon after our parley. He stared daggers when I chanced by, but seemed content to let it at that and get feted by the local highbrows.

I found the Sweeney triplets easy enough. They were playing Meany's farm hands off against the smithy's boys coy as can be. Twinkle in their eyes, those girls were as clever as they were pretty, and I pity the man that married any one of them. Poor bastard will wind up toiling like a rented mule to keep that smile beaming.

52

Upstairs, downstairs, front and back yards, I combed every knot, crowd and cluster twice. I even skirted the barley calling his name. No sign of Paddy.

Two hours later, the sunset had poured molten glory over the western sky but the party showed no mind for slowing. The evening was flush with good folks, free drink, and food, but all I could see was an empty sock, an absent friend, and a royal cur itching to eunuchize me before stringing up my carcass like a gutted deer.

Trying to help, Mayor Tom didn't.

He slipped away from the head table long enough to find me pacing Teagan's front yard. I took a slice of comfort at the thought of Kane enduring Angus' war stories.

Party noises drifted from the back. A lip-locked couple shimmied in the shadows of a nearby doorway. The Mayor stood like he was taking in fresh air, but I could feel he was wound tighter than a clock spring.

"What's this about treasure out of the Teats?" he asked evenly.

Talking had already earned me enough trouble. I stared miserably at the mud on my boots.

"Sweet Jesus, have mercy!" He snorted, incredulous. "Are you gone daft as Paddy?"

He reined in his temper before he spoke again. "Apparently the Queen Mother herself is clutched up over the Meechum's passing."

I swiveled and stared up at him. "Over Meechum Fade?"

He nodded curtly. "'Solicitous' is the royal word, seeing he'd been captain of her guard and all." He fished his pipe and matches from a vest pocket. "Would to God someone is half this solicitous at my funeral."

"And you believe it?"

A match flared, brightening the mayor's lined face and white hair. "Don't matter what I believe, does it now? Who's a lowly, bog-trotting mayor to question a royal concern?"

"Man's a right bastard," I muttered.

"Since you asked," he continued, "what I *don't* believe is Officer Odhran Kane riding all this way for a tearful of sniffles over a fresh grave. Or that the Queen Mother wanted to throw us a bash."

"Then why's he here?"

Mayor Tom's thoughts strained like dogs on a leash. "Call me mad, but by everything Kane's *not* saying, I suspect Her Majesty's knickers are in a serious twist and he's here to sort it out," he finally said.

The image of that muddy locket leapt to mind, its scripty etching, the lass inside it... I clamped down, scared even thinking it too loud would call her forth, bring her walking out of the dark street.

My bones knew the answer to my next question even as the words left my mouth. "What the devil would Carn have could get the Queen Mother worked up so?"

Mayor Tom sucked his pipe angrily. "Damned if I know, but you and Paddy are in Kane's sights."

Paddy. A wave of guilt soured my stomach. He was about all I had left in this world. I'd never forgive myself if he came to harm.

The mayor gripped my shoulder. "Dunno what possessed you to spin shite to that nasty badger," he whispered fiercely, "but you better wind yer neck in. I stood for you; said you and Paddy were good lads underneath, but Kane's settled your tale stinks more than an air biscuit. And has less heft."

He leaned in close. "He's taking an account of Fade's shop before he leaves for Daire tomorrow. For your sake, he better find something, 'cause he's reporting to the Queen Mother. And true guilt or innocence won't enter much into it."

With that, he left me.

A moan from the doorway meant the action had turned hot and heavy. I trudged off wishing I could at least hold Teagan's hand.

I needed a good plan soon, but with evening here and no Paddy, I settled for a stupid one quick.

***

I told Kane it had been a sack of valuables, and a sack of valuables it would be.

Weasel a window, rifle the glass case for a couple chains here, a watch there... Nick some shinier trifles from the fat man's inventory, then stuff 'em in burlap on a back shelf. Wasn't genius, but the only fella could prove otherwise was wheedling St. Peter for the password through the Pearly Gates.

55

Fade's affair was going like a house on fire, and the more ale and cider flowed, the louder his praises were sung. At this rate, the big man would find himself canonized by morning.

Saint Meechum, Patron of Surly Mutes and Girthy Pawnbrokers. I smiled at the thought of Vicar Duffy working that into the liturgy.

As I slipped towards the edge of town, I hoped the Vicar had kept up on his praying. Breaking into a dead man's house to prop up a lie is like planting a feather and hoping to grow a hen. This scheme sure didn't smack of wisdom. But it was all I had. And like my Da used to say, you work what you got.

I hit the crossroad, hopped 'Tater' Gooley's fence, minced through his pasture until I spied Fade's house. Moonlight limed the cellar shutter behind a tangle of white dead-nettle and fern. I felt the candle stub and matches in my pocket, rubbed my thumb across the coarse gunny sack, then gathered my courage.

The wind sighed across the fields, music and laughter trickled down the lanes and between the houses. Easy in, easy out, I told myself. Get Kane down the road, then there'll be plenty of time to sort out the locket and the mystery lass. Even if it means carting down to Dubhlinn to pawn her trouble onto the next unsuspecting sod.

A deep breath, a dozen steps, then I knelt like prayers. I flicked open my penknife and went to work on the latch.

***

Fade's shop might have been clutter and shambles, but his cellar was neater than a cornfield at early spring. Shelves, bins, boxes, everything in smart rows, straight up, swept and labeled. Not a cobweb in sight. A trace of the old soldier, like his tone the other night.

A set of solid steps rose to a sturdy oak door above me. To be honest, even though Fade's casket got roped into a hole, my nerves cooked up the image of him all uniformed, waiting on his stool, jeweler's loupe sighting down a fancy wheel lock pistol. I guess dreaming of dead girls wasn't healthy for the imagination.

But it came down to a promise; I'd sworn to look after Paddy. This was my shot at saving his skin and mine.

I shoved my frights aside and went up, holding the taper in front of me like a charm.

The door was unlocked. I shivered as it creaked open. The room yawned open, dark as a tar pit. Fade's merchandise loomed in snaggy, black mounds. I cupped the candle stub and risked a quick lift, then seeing where I was, promised Jesus, Mary, Joseph I'd go to church for a year.

I was at the back, half a dozen paces from the counter.

The glass in the case wavered feebly from the tiny flame, the contents gleaming like fish darting through murky water. I pulled out the gunny sack and went to work.

Four rings, three gold chains and a two pair of mossy copper bridle bits weren't much of a trove, but any more would leave the case pecked over. I considered a pocket watch or two, but clockworks in the Teats made as much sense as wings on a pig. I jingled the bag;

nowhere near six silver worth. Then I remembered the canes. Or rather the cane heads.

Fade kept a bushel of walking sticks inside the front door, a number topped with ornate bronze heads. Heavy enough to stun a horse, worn shiny smooth from decades of palm oils, they were an easy pass as olden bits. A quick twist, ditch the sticks and they'd fill out the bag nice.

I groped my way forward and was wrenching on a knobby wolf's head when Angus' voice came through the door. It was mumbled by drink and groveling, but the response was clear as a bell.

"That's why you brought a lantern," Odhran Kane snapped. "This *treasure* should be easy to find, no?"

Keys rattled at the door.

I snuffed the wick and scooted back behind the counter just as the door banged open.

"Och, all respect Mister Kane, Fade was a bit of a pack rat. Shop's a jumble, all nooks and crannies. I really think the morning would a better time ta—"

"I'm not staying in this hovel a moment longer than necessary," Kane said. "I'll make a determination now, then drag those two to Daire in the morning. Did Meechum have a strongbox?"

A snuffle. "Can't say, sir. Mr. Fade, erm... Mr. Fade ne'er said much ta anyone. No friends in Carn to speak of."

"No surprise there," I heard Kane mutter. Boots clomped on the wood plank floor. Stopped. "Do you smell smoke?"

My stones shriveled. I stuffed the candle stub in my pocket.

58

"Smell smoke, sir?" Angus quavered.

"Yes," Kane hissed. "Smoke. Candle wax."

"Not candles, sir. It's this." A rusty creak and there was a lurch of new shadows as Angus raised his lantern. "Wick's a mite greasy."

I caught the rasp of steel pulled from a scabbard. "Lift that, shire reeve," Odhran Kane ordered. "Higher."

Shadows reeled on the back wall. Hard shapes and the unnatural stretch of a man with a sword. "Higher," Kane said. "Stay with me."

Boots tromped again, accompanied by a shuffling step. Above me, light crazed off the glass in the case.

"Keep that steady, you old fool!"

The dark wedge of the open basement door mocked me, mere feet away, but I'd never make it. Footsteps louder with each pace. I curled in on myself and started praying.

HelpGodPleasePleaseI'msorryforeverythingI'veeverdonebad. Don'tlethimfindme.PleaseI'llnever do—

"What the devil is this?" A voice suddenly shouted out. I near wet myself.

It was Mayor Tom.

Kane sighed like he was addressing a child. "I'm inspecting Meechum's merchandise, as we discussed."

"We agreed I'd be present for the scrutinizing. Tomorrow morning."

"Early start—early finish," Kane sniffed. "I want to be riding before noon. I decided to search now."

The mayor's incredulity was hard as stone. "In the pitch dark with drawn steel? What are you playing at?"

"I thought I saw someone."

"Thought he whiffed bee's wax," Angus added helpfully.

"I'll give you a tot of wax, if you like. On a sealed letter, complaining of your disregard for my office, not to mention common sense and decency," Mayor Tom concluded. "Leave out now. We'll be here once there's sun for a proper search."

There was a damn long hush, Kane's decision weighing in the air. Then the boots strode away.

I started breathing again after the door slammed and the lock thunked fast.

***

I lingered long as I dared, fumbling a second bronze knob and a handful of tarnished flatware into the sack, which I stuffed on a knee-shelf behind Fade's counter. I prayed it was enough. It would have to be. I got my lifetime's fill of lurking and larceny that night.

All I wanted was my bed, the quilt over my head, and for it all to go away.

I dashed through the crossroads, one eye over my shoulder, on down the lane until the boxy lines of Widow Halloran's house rose against the charcoal of the starry night. I stopped stock still.

The second-floor corner window was lit up, blazing like an oven mouth. Same as Fades the other night.

Paddy's room.

My heels bruised my arse racing to the house. I slipped on the stairs, smacked my noggin, scrambled all fours the rest of the way.

My eyes were tearing when I burst through the door. "Don't you be touching him, you ghouly bitch—"

Paddy was perched on the end of his bed, locket in hand. Gold glinted, the scratchy writing writhing there in his palm. A punched tin lamp glowed on his side table. Fireflies in a jar would give more light. There was no sign of a blaze.

"What the—?" I blurted.

He didn't even look up. Just sat still as a statue, gazing at that locket.

Forehead throbbing, heart in my throat a second time that night, I snatched the damned thing out of his hand. "Oi! I turned the town over looking for you."

Paddy stared like he'd never laid eyes on me before.

I cuffed him across the head. "The shite I wade through for you, and this is how you treat me?"

He welled up, started to speak.

I was too steamed to give way. "Serves you right," I yelled. "Pinching goods out of my cupboard and dropping off like that." I stuck a finger in his face. "I's just near stabbed on account of you."

A hundred questions jigged on the tip of my tongue, each shoving for first place. I was about to let 'em run when Paddy spoke.

"It's always night there," he whispered. "She's lost in th' dark."

My mouth went dry. "Always night where?"

His face screwed up to cry. He went on like he didn't hear me. "She only dreams the world now, aching for a way back."

"Who?"

"The lass in the picture, Magalie. Someone killed her. "He looked strayed as a little lamb. "I just went to help."

Hackles rose down my neck. I thrust the locket at him. "This ain't for you, mate. Got me?"

His shoulders hunched.

"I'm telling you true," I pressed. "It's bad, Paddy. It's... unnatural."

"She needs me—"

"No," I shouted. "You *needs* to leave it be. O'right?"

I wrung his shoulder when he wouldn't answer. "You mind me here! This ain't some trinket."

His brows took a mulish set. "She was crying, so I went."

"Went where?"

"Back to the little hill where we dug it up."

I was so frothed, my words stumbled over each other. "You're thick as an anvil, you big-footed galute," I said. "Useless as a back pocket on a shirt, ya dumb—"

Paddy's face lumped up."I ain't dumb."

62

I clenched the locket 'til the edges dug in my skin. "Aye, you are," I retorted. "You're... you're *traipsing* 'round the woods alone. You know you aren't supposed to do that. Why the devil'd you go?"

Paddy thrust his chin out. "She called *me* is why!" He was up and at me before I could blink, jabbing fingers in my chest. "*Me*. She called me."

I fish-mouthed, tottered back a pace.

Paddy had always had been a big lad. We called him "Bear Baby" all growing up, but he'd never so much as raised a hand to me. Ever. This worried me more than Kane. More than the girl.

He towered over me, raring to scrap. "She needs me. *Me*."

I found my voice when my back hit the doorpost. "She ain't real," I explained slow. "She's a *ghost,* Paddy. A shade."

"She ain't," he glared.

I raised my hands, looked him dead in the eye, serious as Vicar Duffy at Lent. "Is, too. And she's witched you."

Paddy stopped up his ears. "Nononono."

I stuck the locket in his face. "This here killed Fade somehow, you get it? *She* killed Fade."

"No. Magalie's nice. She fancies me," Paddy shot back.

"She's a demon, mate. An evil fae."

His face reddened. "She said I'm the only one can help her."

"Bah."

"You're making this up 'cause she called me and not you," Paddy shouted.

"Oi! She called me too!

"Called you?" He stopped, suddenly fuddled. "When?"

"Last night. Only I dreamed her crying in the woods. Went to the same spot."

The news sagged him. "So she asked you to help, too?"

Memory flashed in my head: cadaverous face, burning eyes, grin like a skull, that screaming neck gash... "No. Not really."

Paddy started jabbering all at once. "Well, she asked my name, name of the town. Even the year, and I told her. Was like she was starving after news. She kept on about the Prince. I said there weren't no Prince, only King Airam and Queen Ysabeau." His brow knit like he was figuring a sum. "She didn't like that. She said—"

Thought of Paddy chatting with Little Miss Bloody Banshee chilled my bones. I cut him off. "It dinnae matter what she said, mate. Listening will only bring grief."

He shook his head like a horse in a cloud of flies. "Why are you so cruel? Poor gal was left like Hansel and Gretel. She just wants back where she belongs."

"What she did to Fade, she can damn well stay where she is."

"No," he pleaded. "Open it. She'll—"

I slid the locket in my vest pocket. "Open it? I've half a mind to chuck it in the river. We got a heap of trouble at our door. The sooner we're free of the bitch, the better, I say."

"No call for names," he groused. "Pretty lass lost like that—"

I stuck my finger in his face. "Clean your ears. She's rotten, and that's all there is to it."

He scowled but I was too busy sorting choices to pay him any mind. The urge to heave the thing from the roof of the mill tugged at me, hard. Drown her like a sack of mangy kittens and be done.

Still, the weight of the thing in my pocket... Gold is gold, after all.

It would be a shame, what we've been dragged through the last two days, to come up empty-handed. Might still be a way to pull a plum out of this.

"Tinker should be by next week," I mused. "But Meany's carting a load of wheat to Daire tomorrow. If I beg a ride..." Providing that bastard Kane didn't run me through first.

"We found it means we're to help her," Paddy insisted.

I used my Da's stern voice to end our controverting. "She's evil, mate. Period. So don't you be coming after it. Right?"

"You feel like that, you shouldn't be touching her locket," he sulked.

I gave him the hairy eyeball. "I mean it. I'll take it from here."

Paddy stood there panting, fists clenching to wring a chicken. I thought he was gonna take a poke at me again, so I braced myself. Then he thought better and turned away.

My heart swelled. Snit all you want, I thought. So long as you're safe. That's all that matters. I reached out to clap him on the back, but he stiffened like a board.

I let my hand fall. "It's late," I said softly. "We'll talk in the morning, right?"

Not a word.

"Fine. Be like that."

I trudged back to my room, suddenly bone tired.

I barely kicked off my boots before I fell on the bed, and I lay there, listening through the wall to Paddy's surly silence. He'd snap out of his brooding eventually, then it'd be like it never happened. My Ma used to say each day was full of new sunshine for him.

Sometimes I wished it were me was touched...

The pieces of his tale didn't tally; who was this haunting Magalie lass? Who was Fade to her? And what would she want in Paddy? A thousand questions swirled thicker than moths at a lantern.

Nightmares or no, I couldn't risk the locket sprouting legs and walking off again, so I slipped it under my mattress, at the foot of my bed. Then spent the rest of the night twitching like a dreaming dog.

Part Four~

The Black Jewel of Senlis

W as quiet that woke me the next morning, an odd shush sitting in the house like a stranger. I sat up. Nothing. Not a creak or squeak from Paddy's room.

Dread pricked my skin and I tumbled out of bed, groping under the mattress like an angry tomcat 'til my fingers hit metal. Locket was still there, snug as a tick. I sat on the floor, one arm buried up to the elbow in sheet telling myself Paddy was washing up or walking off his sulk.

Under the mattress, my finger traced the thorny script on the cover over and over. Spiral in, spiral out, spiral in... The gold was cold, the graven letters scratchy. Sleep had shoved away my worry last night, but it barged back in soon as my eyes opened.

He said her name was Magalie.

Not Gaelic. A foreign name for a foreign lass.

Magalie—you simper or screech at me, but you're kittens and honey for sweet dumb Paddy...

Spiral out, spiral in, spiral out—

Magalie, is this a verse or a curse graven in your strange tongue?

Maybe it depends which way you read it. Like a bad coin toss, had Fade guessed wrong, but Paddy chanced it right?

My bones said no.

I withdrew my hand.

Magalie, time to get you on your way.

Meany's wagons would be rumbling to Daire at noon. I'd off the locket there. The city's pawnshops were nooked in the narrow alleys near the Market Street Wharf, sailors and dockmen a steady source of items need turned to copper. Wouldn't get half its real worth, but that was fine by me. Screaming, dreaming Maggie could find another lover by the sea. I'd be back in Carn by night, my world back to the regular order of things.

Suddenly Odhran Kane's oily mug rose in my mind. Did he find the sack? Had it worked? Wouldn't he be here if it hadn't? Truth was there'd be no leaving 'til I'd faced him. Skipping town would seal my guilt in his eyes, sure as sure. Fear scratched in me like mice in the walls and I earnestly hoped Vicar Duffy had kept up on his prayers.

Propping up my courage, I rubbed the sand from my eyes, made my bed, then pulled on the cleanest clothes I had. I considered taking the locket, but left it under my mattress at the last minute. It had stayed put all night and I sure didn't want it on me when I faced Kane. I'd come back for it later.

Decision made and stomach rumbling, I squared my shoulders and did what I always do when I need fortitude and food; went to find Teagan.

Carn's streets were quiet and groggy, smelling faintly of morning dew and stale beer. The day would be slow to start, everyone being well potted after Fade's send-off.

Almost everyone that is; I found Teagan's bright-eyed and beautiful cousins, Shaelyn and Maerin, mucking out the tavern.

They were on the porch throttling mops when I trudged up the walk.

"She's not here," Maerin called.

"At her Ma's," Shaelyan said before I asked. Both of them stood there grinning at me, all buckets, brooms, and reckless red hair.

"What's so funny?" I asked.

Maerin shrugged innocently. "Oh nothing. Just that you're the second one this morning."

I opened my mouth again, but Shaelyn interjected. "Bradan. Came by, hat in hand, hoping for a chat and a cuppa. Bit unsteady on his feet, but he had something on his mind."

My mood soured. Bradan Magee. Blacksmith's eldest. Tall, square jaw, shoulders like an ox yoke, wits to match. County Crae girls went all swoony around him. Never saw why, myself.

"So?" I grumped.

"Told him to try back later," Maerin stated matter-of-factly. "Said she was still asleep."

"Which she was," Shaelyn noted.

"Aye. 'Cept not here." Maerin returned.

"Where then?" I burst out.

"At her Ma's." Maerin laughed. "Like we told you."

Shaelyn suddenly fixed me with a new look. "Where you off to, up so early?"

I puffed up a bit. "Helping Meany get a load to Daire."

Maerin's emerald eyes narrowed. "The city, eh? You fetching a ring?"

I flushed. Bloody small town. "Errr... I, uh, am doing some business. Well, that is to say..." My voice trailed off.

The girls' eyes sparkled at my discomfort. Finally Maerin waved me off. "She's probably up now. If you're quick, you'll get breakfast."

I rushed off, silver bells of laughter chasing me down the lane.

***

Ma Cooney's was on the west side of town, across town square, a pair of limewash dogtrot cottages with new thatch and a generous kitchen garden, all surrounded by an ancient stone wall veiled in violets and pansies. As I neared the Civic House, I heard careful voices and kettles whistling. Folk were rousing now, treading gingerly into a new day. I walked faster, hoping Teagan was awake, Bradan was back to snoring, and Ma Cooney had the stove lit.

Head down, I was working how and how much I'd tell her. Delicate thing to know what parts to leave out and still get a true eye on the situation. Especially one like this.

My belly reminded me it was empty, so I picked up the pace. With no mind to anything but my worries, I never saw Kane coming.

Bastard chested that big black stallion right into me, sent me arse over teakettle. The horse snickered. Kane let out an ugly giggle. "If you bruised Brom, I'll whip you within an inch of your life."

He loomed over me from the saddle, one hand white-knuckled on the hilt of his sword, the other holding reins dainty as a china cup.

"Br—Brom?" I managed.

"My horse, Flood. Worth ten times you."

I sat up and wiped the mud from my sleeves and face. Kane sneered down, a nasty thought twitching behind his hard little eyes. I cast about to bolt, but there was nowhere he and that damn horse couldn't run me down in five steps.

Kane must have seen the frantic in my face. He laughed. "The guilty flee when no one pursues."

I bit my tongue and held his gaze, heart hammering in my chest.

"We found your bag of junk," he continued. "Your *treasure*. At first, I didn't believe it, but your mayor insisted. Proof of innocence, he said."

Kane sniffed like he'd caught a whiff of awful. "Meechum must have gone soft, giving that kind of money for rubbish. That's what living with you bogtrotters does, apparently."

Leather creaked as he glanced back to the Civic House. Mayor Tom watched us from the steps, anxious. Angus squinted beside him. Kane deliberately released his sword and offered them a cool nod.

"Innocent or not, I'd love to watch you kick out a hangman's jig," he whispered. "But I can't get out of this village fast enough. So I'm leaving you to your cabbage-gorging life, Flood."

Kane leaned over in the saddle, pulling the reins. The horse Brom twisted his big head toward me, bared his teeth. "If I ever lay eyes on you or your idiot cousin again," Kane hissed. "I'll flay you alive, then throw your corpses on a dung heap. Hear me?"

I nodded.

He straightened up. "Now get out of my way." He flicked the reins.

I managed to roll to one side as he and his brute thundered off.

I stood and wiped my hands on my trousers until my knees stopped knocking. Damn near thing, that was.

"You o'right?" Mayor Tom called.

No, I thought, but waved weakly and went on my way.

Smoke was threading from Ma Cooney's chimney, the yard wreathed in the heavy warmth of fresh baked bread and bacon grease. The shutters were open at the kitchen window and I heard crockery clattering, a spoon scraping a pan. Out back, linen flapped on a drying line.

I breathed it in and a yearning heaved in my chest, coiling around my heart like a sad, half-remembered song. It hurt in a good way and I stood with my hand on the gate, scared but perfectly still, lest I scare the feeling off.

It surged through me like a wind, then I went and knocked on the door.

***

Ma Cooney bustled me in before going out back to wash up. Teagan was in the kitchen, hair down, fresh-faced and pretty as a peach in her rumpled night dress. I fumbled over how to begin as she brewed up a kettle of Barry's. She read my nerves, but let it be. Which was fine, seeing as I didn't make it to the bottom of my first cup before it tumbled out in a rush: the locket, Fade's that night, the horror on his face, that little smile, my dream, now the mess with Paddy...

It stopped fast as it begun, and I sat there worried she'd think me babbling mad. Seeing murdered girls and spooks can earn you a long stay in a small room at St. Cormac's monastery, sipping gruel under the eye of concerned clergy.

Teagan studied my face without saying a word. It went on so long I squirmed on my stool.

"You believe me, don'cha?" I asked sheepishly.

She blew a stray lock of hair out for her face and nodded slowly. "Trouble finds the pair of you like fleas find dogs. Almost natural, you stumbling into weirdness."

"Really?"

I couldn't decide whether I was grateful or surprised, she took it so casual. I wasn't keen on her matching me with trouble though.

"Not an every-day sort of tale, though?" I said defensively.

Teagan thunked a plate of black pudding, toast, eggs and bacon in front of me. "Declan darlin', this isn't the most peculiar thing that's ever floated past me."

I waited but she didn't expound. "You need to talk with my Ma," was all she said.

I mumbled grace and took up my fork. "'Bout what?" I asked, just as Ma Cooney came through the back door.

Teagan aimed a wooden spoon. "She'll tell you herself."

"Tell 'im what?" Ma Cooney rasped.

"What you said last night. About Meechum Fade."

Her ma's face went flat and hard as an iron skillet.

"Go on," Teagan insisted. "Declan was the one to find him. Tell him what you told me last night."

Ma Cooney shook her head. "The past is best left there. No good comes of digging it up."

"It's truth, not slander, Ma. Besides, I already told him about the white lady's headstone."

"Don't make it his business," she snorted back. "Besides, it's not proper to speak ill of the dead."

"Ma, he needs to hear the clincher. It's pertinent."

"*Im*pertinent is what you are," she snapped.

I sopped egg with a hank of toast. "What clincher?"

Ma Cooney and Teagan locked eyes like goats butting heads. I got half ready to duck under the table.

"That Meechum Fade," Teagan began.

The silence built up. "Was a murderer," Ma Cooney finished.

"Soldier does his share of killing," I philosophied carefully. "Can't all of it be just."

The morning sun was streaming through the leaded glass, drenching the table and floor in pools of warm gold. Ma Cooney stared out into the yard. "I'm speaking 'bout that day in the woods, you numpty."

I leaned forward. "Fade was one of the soldiers?"

"He was *the* soldier," she said.

I was still thick from lack of sleep. "The soldier?"

"The one slit the girl's throat," she said gruffly.

I recalled Teagan's story: maid and a lady having a row, a gesture, then a soldier — a big man stepping up behind the lass, quick and quiet. "That was Fade?" I choked out.

Brown, gnarled hands started worrying the tea towel in her apron. "It was almost twenty years on when he came back to Carn on the Crown's pension," Ma Cooney explained. "He'd grayed quite a bit. Had a beard and a belly, but it was him, sure as sure. The one I seen that day."

"Why didn't you report him?" I asked.

"Me?" Ma Cooney laughed. "Accuse a retired officer from the queen's guard, a landowner, a decade after the fact?" She shook her head again. "Reaping the whirlwind, that."

"But murdering an innocent— "

76

"I was a child when I saw it. Without proof, it wouldn't hold water. Besides, Fade was spreading money around, running his shop. Even if it were only copper. Buys a pile of good will, that does."

"But you're saying Meechum Fade cut a maiden's throat on a noble woman's orders."

Another load of tension silted up in the room. "Not just a noble woman—" Teagan prompted.

"Queen Niamh," her mother said.

I gaped to catch flies.

Ma Cooney raised a trembling right hand. "True as true, the lady was Queen Niamh."

"Who was the lass?" I gulped.

"Can't say," she replied too quickly.

"But you've got a notion."

Another pause, then a nod.

"Who then?"

"The Black Jewel of Senlis." She spoke so soft I barely heard the words.

I looked to Teagan. She shrugged.

Ma Cooney cleared her throat and started putting vegetables back into her garden basket. "I shouldn't be saying any of this. Was long ago. Got no bearing on today."

"It just might, Ma," Teagan urged gently. "It's what we're trying to sort out. Who was this 'Jewel of Senlis'?"

"*Black* Jewel," Ma Cooney corrected. She stopped fussing with turnips and gathered herself. "Your father—God rest his soul—

and I were minding the inn in those days. Every trader and traveler jabbered on about them. From Gaul they were, the Morreaux family. Father, mother, daughter—distant relations of the king. High born but not too high, if you catch my meaning. Rich in name but little else."

"What were they doing in Éire?" I asked.

"Fleeing famine was the story. Four years of bleak winters and dry springs on the continent. Desperate times make desperate folk. Entire regions were starving, sick... Lots of new graves scraped in the parched earth of Gaul and Normandy, so the family came begging favor of King Arnaw. Wanting land. A fresh start."

"Must be nice, a fief on tap from your cousin's uncle," Teagan said lightly.

Ma Cooney shook her head, suddenly grim. "But there were whispers of another reason."

I tried jesting her down a notch. "Always is. Who'd we tear down if there weren't those above us?"

She crossed herself before looking me square in the face. "They were dark whispers. And bloody reasons."

A powerful dread crept over me, but Teagan spoke up. "Like?"

"Like both Morreaux' sons had died earlier that year. Family blamed cholera but traders heard... they'd been burned at the stake."

"What?" I exclaimed.

"Aye, and the family was really fleeing the Black Friars, not famine. Said they'd seen a warrant nailed to church doors charging them with heresy and unholy consorting."

"Unholy consorting?"

Ma Cooney glanced about before answering. "With the Devil. Witchcraft."

"Load of tosh," Teagan said after a second. "Go against the grain, those are the first likely words out of a bishop's mouth."

"Aye," Ma Cooney allowed. "Except drought came here the next year. So did the Fichti. And that was the summer they killed Prince Aedh."

Teagan and I were silent. Her ma continued. "The daughter was the eye of the storm. Folks said she was a rare thing, with raven hair and looks beyond words. A beauty, but a strange, dark one, like midnight in the deep woods."

I took a sudden interest in my eggs. Her description sat too close for comfort.

"Folks claimed she had a presence, an eerie set to her," she said carefully. "That to gaze into her eyes was like looking into deep wells."

I squirmed on my stool again. "You certain it was this Senlis m'amselle in the woods?"

Ma Cooney sucked her teeth. "Not like I strolled up and asked her, did I? But the hair and the rest of it sure fit."

"What would she be doing with the Queen up north?" Teagan mused. "Quite the ride from Dubhlinn."

"Prince Aram was sotted with her, that's why," her ma replied. "Whole kingdom knew. He followed her around like a puppy. Every royal son from Corcaigh to Daire was sniffing after her but rumor was he was talking marriage."

"And with his brother dead, he was heir to the Emerald Throne," I noted. "She'd be queen."

"Exactly," Ma Cooney said. "Bed her, sure, but marriage? The King and Queen were dead set against *that*. Penniless lass brings no gold to the table. No alliance, no land. Add a pot full of rumors and scandal, it wasn't going to happen."

I had an ugly feeling as to where this story landed, but I asked hoping it wouldn't. "So?"

"So what?"

"What did happen?" Teagan demanded. "Obvious he didn't marry her. Queen Ysabeau is Welsh."

"King Arnaw refused a land grant," Ma Cooney said simply. "We heard the Morreaux family up and sailed to England. Right after that carriage passed though here, in fact. News mongers claimed the Black Jewel of Senlis left Prince Airam high and dry. Dumped him for better prospects. Lad moped for months. That's what they said, anyway."

"But you're persuaded that was her in the woods Fade killt?" I asked again.

Ma Cooney pursed her lips. "Can't prove it but I'd swear in my bones before God it was." She nodded. "Aye, it was."

She paused then and looked me over narrowly. "Why are you so keen on this? You got a bee in your trousers?"

I looked back, head suddenly empty as a busted bucket. "I, erm. Well, with Fade passing and the party, I was, umm—"

Teagan came to my rescue. "He's out of sorts, Declan is. Finding Fade dead, this Kane fellow talking up his younger days soldiering. It got him curious, is all."

Her ma harrumphed and shuffled past us toward the front room. I threw Teagan a grateful look, then a worry hit me like a rock.

"Her name," I called after Ma Cooney. "D'you remember that Senlis' lass's name?"

"Of course I do," she replied. "I'm old, not daft. Magalie, it was. Magalie Morreaux de Senlis,"

My heart went crossways at those words.

I made hasty goodbyes and ducked out, walking as fast as I dared without drawing attention. The sun was beaming, townsfolk were stirring, trading stories and bashful smiles about the previous night. Birds sang and flitted through an azure sky smooth and perfect as the first day in Eden.

But all I could see was that tiny smile and those terrible blank eyes.

Magalie. Magalie Morreaux de Senlis.

Back home, I climbed the stairs calling for Paddy. No answer.

I hesitated on the top landing. The door to my room was open a notch, the whole house heavy and silent. The morning's stiff silence was back.

"Paddy?" I creaked my door wider.

And lost my breath.

On the floor lay a pile of rumpled linen. Beside it, Widow Halloran.

Her face was a mask of fear, frozen and unblinking. One hand clutched her chest, the other held the locket.

The cover was open and Magalie was smiling up at me again.

Part Five ~

Certain as the Moon Above

The churchyard was packed with mourning black and sorrow, all of Carn standing silent in the bright morning sun.

Vicar Duffy made the sign of the cross, signaling the blacksmiths' boys to lower the coffin. Ropes hissed across their shoulders, slithered in their grip, until the dull thud at the bottom. A new headstone, smooth and unblemished as a baby's cheek, canted in the green grass by the fence, epitaph imminent. Old Whitey Quigg insisted on more time to chisel something fancy for the Widow. "As is only proper," he said.

The first shovelful of dirt hit the lid. Behind me, someone sobbed.

"*Requiem aeternam dona eis, Domine,*" the Vicar intoned. "*Et lux perpetua luceat ei.*"

Grant them eternal rest, O Lord. And let perpetual light shine upon her.

That I knew the meaning was due to the woman in the box, God rest her soul. Truth be told, any sense of letters or figures I had was down to Widow Halloran. It was her who convinced my Da to let me go on to secondaries, who strong-armed Mayor Tom into buying my books, who told my Ma over and over again I showed promise, despite all the trouble I got myself into. And it was her who took me in after the fever took them.

The spades were swinging now, the lid near covered. I cleared my throat and cuffed away a tear. Holy water pattered down on newly turned soil. "*Requiescat in pace.*"

Rest in Peace.

Behind me, the crowd murmured "Amen."

Everyone held still until the dirt mounded, then filed down the road two by two or in muted clumps, sniffling and clutching arms. Carn might have Vicar Duffy and Major Tom for all things ecclesiastical or civic, but as headmistress of the only school in County Crae, Widow Halloran had been the final authority on grammar, mathematics and manners for three generations. She'd left her mark on most everyone assembled, and not just from occasional raps on the knuckles.

Now she was dead and Magalie was to blame; murderous Magalie Morreaux popping out of her locket and causing all this grief.

The picture of the Widow lying on the floor like a broken stick doll, gold disc winking in her palm, mask of nightmares on her face gnawed at me like termites.

I should have taken a mallet to the damn thing, chucked the pieces in the river.

But no.

Vicar Duffy says it's a mortal sin to pray to the Devil, but I was biting my tongue so's not to beg Old Nick to hurry up and take her screaming, smiling, lying, undying soul to the furnace.

The shame of it burned me.

Paddy and I walked down the lane wrapped in all that somber hush, townsfolk flowing around us. Nothing passed between us. We hadn't said more than a handful of words to each other since yesterday. There'd been no time.

He'd cried when I told him, carried the body downstairs to Morton and Figg so they could load her into their black carriage. Big galute tucked her in like she was asleep. I tried to talk to him then, to explain what happened, but he wasn't in a listening mood. Not about the Widow, and certainly not about Magalie.

The locket was in the attic, on a rafter under the gable end. I'd squirreled it away until I had a better mind on what to do with it.

For the second time in as many days, Teagan's inn hosted a wake. Difference this go-round was all Carn pitched in. No talk of outlay, no thought to cost. Men dragged kegs up from their cellars, blew the dust off single malts they'd stashed away against cold winter nights, all without a second thought. Less than an hour after the service, a score of women set heaping platters to the tables, pots of bubbling stew, and mounds of rolls still steaming from their ovens.

County Crae folk are proper-minded, poor in gold but big on horse sense and common courtesy. Paying their respects to Fade was only natural, and no one turns down a free meal. This time however, the town's grief was palpable, not purchased, the generosity characteristic rather than conscripted. We were sending off one of our own.

At the inn, Paddy gave me a nod, then lined up for stew. The set of his eyes told me he still wasn't up for a chat. I was too heavy, too fuddled to insist, so I nodded back with a determination to find him after. We had to sit down and hash things out before they festered any further.

Teagan found me at the bar. "You okay?"

"No."

She waved Maerin over to grab her tray of empty bowls, then plumped down beside me. Her nearness lit a kernel of sadness in my stomach like I was faint with some kind of hunger. I gripped the bar to keep from falling onto her shoulder.

She looked me in the eye, concerned and soft. "How's Paddy taking it?"

"Barely said a word." I shook my head miserably. "He's keeping his cards close to his chest. It's like he doesn't want to talk to me."

Teagan tried joking. "No surprise, folks not feeling chatty 'round you," she said lightly. "You 'prenticing under *An Bás*, and all. Second body in a week. Still, the *shuffle 'em to the hereafter* trade is steady work."

The memory of the open locket in the Fade's hand, in the Widow's hand, flashed in my head. "I'm not laughing, Tea." I gulped back a sob. "It's all my fault."

She gripped my arm. "Och! I was only teasing, Dec. Don't you beat yourself up. She was getting on and it's only bad luck, you finding her—"

"No," I stammered. "It was..."

Teagan arched an eyebrow.

"Her," I confessed. "Magalie."

"Magalie...?" Teagan's gaze narrowed. "You mean—"

"I mean the lass in the locket *is* Magalie from Senlis."

"Go on," she cried.

"Makes sense, don't it? We dug it out the place of her murder. She told Paddy her name the other night, and when your Ma said it, I rushed home. Only it was too late; Widow H found it under my sheets. She opened it."

"Under your sheets?" She looked ready to hit me. "Are you mad?"

"Well, yes. And no." I shrugged.

"Why kill the Widow?" Teagan demanded.

"I dunno," I answered. "Not like I got a handle on this heebie-jeebie stuff. Maybe she just got in the way. "

"But you opened it, right?"

"Aye, but..." I thought back to that morning in the woods, to my dream, then Paddy the other night. "Four of us opened it. Two are dead."

"But two are alive. And you're one of them," Teagan said. "That's gotta mean something."

"Maybe." I held my breath, studying her face. "What I don't get," I said slowly, "is why I got shrieks and blood, but she's all coquette with Paddy."

Teagan blinked, looking at me like the answer was plain as the nose on my face. "She wants something is why," she explained. "It's what girls do."

"What? You're only nice when you're after something, is that it?"

"No. Not all of us and not always." She reached over the bar and fished up a bottle of beer, set it in front of me. "Think on the Sweeny Triplets though. This... *Magalie* is all cute with Paddy 'cause he has something she wants."

"Love him to pieces, but he's not the full shilling. Can't keep two pennies long enough to rub 'em together, let alone much else."

She frowned. "He's kept you as a friend, hasn't he?"

I reddened. "That's not what I meant."

"Well I dunno *what* she wants," Teagan said firmly. "But it don't have a happy ending. You have to look after him."

"I have all my life," I protested. "Why do you think I'm humping bales for Meany? I'm down to Daire to pawn the bloody thing off soon as."

Teagan looked dubious. "That wise, passing a ghosty girl's poison on to someone else?"

I clenched my fists on the counter top. "I'm wise enough to know she's brought enough grief, and I want it—her—far away as can be."

89

Teagan raised her hands and stood up. "Your call, Declan darlin'. I'd be on my way to the smithy's forge myself. Give the wench a taste of locket-hell."

"But it's gold."

Teagan stood up and started back to the kitchen. "And that's more important?"

It is to me, I thought, but kept that to myself.

"Wait. I need to ask you something," I called out.

She came back and waited for me to speak.

I hemmed and hawed, working up a good turn of phrase. Finally, "You think I'm losing my mind?"

She was startled. "No, why do you ask?"

"Well," I struggled. "All this talk of evil spirits and dreams, you being a regular church-goer, I worried you'd think it a load of tosh and blasphemy."

The way she looked brought heat to my cheeks. She stared so long I looked away.

"Declan Flood," she finally said, "there's plenty that's dark and terrible in this world. Why do you think the Son of God came?"

With that, she walked away.

And that, I reasoned, was a damn fine answer.

I spent the next hour nursing my beer, thinking on what Teagan said; about dark things, about Magalie, about her *wanting* something.

Neighbors, various and sundry, milled around me, each with a wry chuckle and story "about the time," but behind the brimming eyes and friendly claps on the back was a wariness. Folks dying, peerage-types poking around, a strangeness on the wind... their world was out of kilter, and they sensed me in the middle of it.

I laughed and hugged and daubed my own tears away, but Magalie's *want* kept gnawing at me. Paddy didn't have a pot to piss in or a window to throw it out of. Barely remembered his name at times. He had nothing worth taking. The big lad's only saving grace was dowsing...

Dowsing.

Ma Cooney's story hit me like a brick; it wasn't the *what* so much as the *who*.

Fade snatched life and love away from her that day in the woods. Revenging on him—that I got. But a royal lady had ordered it—and Ma Cooney had named Queen Niamh.

Now Queen Mother Niamh, ensconced in a hall on the hills over Daire.

Daire.

I ran outside looking for Meany's wagons; they were gone. And so was Paddy.

***

I stole Mayor Tom's horse.

Of course Paddy found the locket; finding things is what he does. I wanted to smack myself for being so stupid. Magalie needed Paddy to find her way to the Queen Mother. And not to beg a boon.

I worked the mare near lather trying to overtake Meany, but he had too great a start on me. Midway on the Letterkenny Road, the sky fell and drizzled piss-warm rain just long enough to raise mud and drench me to the bone. I trotted through the Bishop's Gate near dusk, arse-sore, soaked, and filthy as a used dishrag.

The walled city of Daire sat on the west bank of the River Foyle, which spilled into the aptly named harbor, Lough Foyle. I saw the canvas-white of sails swaying over the rooftops near the docks. On the river's east side, St. Colmcille's large stone church mothered a mob of wattle and daubs amidst neat fields of barley and vegetables. Beyond them, a grove of gnarled oaks, ancient and rooted as Druids, stretched up into the hills. The sun was slipping away, drawing light after it, all the belfries ringing Angelus into the gloom. The moon hadn't risen, but in the deepening west, early stars winked fierce and bright as worm holes in the floorboards of heaven. Lurking at the edge of the Market Square, I could make out Meany and his wagon. He was fixing to return home. No sign of Paddy.

I gathered a few askance looks asking after the Queen Mother's residence—not being the picture of propriety—but a rag-seller finally pointed me north. "Minding the harbor entrance. West side, at the very end of Greencastle Road," she croaked. "Big hall, white as snow with a red slate roof. You can't miss it."

I rode north, night dropping hard and fast, part of me hoping I would.

Half a mile from the Point, I tied the Mayor's horse in a stand of Wych Elm a stone's throw off the road. Far enough to be hidden for the night, close enough to be found in case things didn't work out. I didn't dwell too long on that—the bald truth of me without anything resembling a *plan* fixed my immediate attention. Tomorrow had its own troubles, the Vicar always said. Skulking along right then in the scrub, I wondered more than once how I got so stupid.

I tried being sly as a fox, but was more a lost cow, bumbling around in the unfamiliar dark, snapping branches and tripping over roots. I dove in the bushes several times as riders and a wagon passed me, but the wind off the sea was shaking the treetops, rushing through the tall grass. That and inky dark were the only reasons I wasn't found out.

Took twice the time it should have, but the road eventually ended. A fat Gibbous moon had climbed over the far landside hills, dappling everything silver and slate, and I could see the ocean heaving on my right, a vast stretch of burnished lead, breathing slowly. Close to the house, I started creeping in earnest.

Crickets chorused in the hills, a thousand wee voices matching the throaty rumble of waves surging up over the cliff edge. The tang of brine stung my eyes, salted my lips. I scouted out a thick patch of hazel on a rise above the Point, ducked in, gathered myself, then peered out... and my heart sank like a stone.

The Queen Mother's residence was more fortified estate than house. I counted three smaller cottages, a stable, small barn, and separate kitchen house, all of it surrounded by a high wall. Her fancy white hall with its ruddy roof was plopped at the back at the cliff. When the old woman had said "minding the harbor" she'd really meant

"near tumbling into it;" her Majesty's manor was perched on the very edge like a cormorant roost.

If that weren't bad enough, it took me spying the soldiers to remember Kane. Odhran Kane, Captain of the Queen Mother's Guard. Mystery to me how I could forget the man slavering to giblet and hang me beside the very Gate I'd passed through earlier that day. My Ma always said I had a good memory, even if it is a bit short.

If there was one person I wouldn't mind introducing to Magalie, it was Kane. Seemed to me the two of them were perfect for each other. Match-made-in-Hades, that was.

The manor's main entrance was closed up with fancy wrought-iron, a guard shack stuck right outside. I could see helmets glinting in torchlight. A straight long shadow in the turf revealed a second path that veered off the main road farther back. It led to a pair of stout wooden doors in the wall near the cliff edge. The servant's entrance.

Sticking to bushes and dark folds on the hill, I skirted around the three sides of Queen Niamh's house. There was no other gate, no breech in the wall, no gardener's shack right up next to it. Not even a tree with overhanging branches.

How in God's name Paddy weaseled his way in there, I had no idea. But in there he was, I knew it certain as the moon above, the sun tomorrow, my own heart beating. If anyone could find a way in, it'd be him. Finding things is what he did. And he would, 'cause that's what that venomous bitch Magalie wanted.

I had the stone cold notion once she'd got what she came for, she'd toss him aside like a stale crust of bread. Between her and Kane, he didn't stand a chance.

Raw from the wind, near chilled to death, I had a powerful dread sitting on me, but courage is being scared and standing up anyway. My best mate was down there and I was the only one to help him.

It was on my second pass around I noticed the drainage ditch. Barely more than a slit in the ground, it ran alongside the servant's footpath and disappeared under the shadows below the wall by the wooden door. It was a long shot but it was better than nothing.

I doubled back, crossed the road, then slithered through the grass, popping up like a jack-in-the-box now and again to search for it. I found it when I tumbled in.

It was the manor's drain; muck and fluids from the kitchen house, the privy, and God knows where else sludged down there.

Shite.

It was such a good idea when it was still an idea.

The stench of rotted food and chamber pots gagged me, watered my eyes 'til I was weeping and snotting like an infant, but I held my breath and crawled.

95

And crawled.

And crawled until I reached the wall.

Near four feet down at the foundation, I made out a rusty iron grate wedged in a stone culvert. By starlight, I saw a gap where the bars were bent and broken. Looked just wide enough.

I lay on my side, reached my arms all the way in and started to shimmy forward.

All that ooze was good for something. I managed my head, then my shoulders, then—slowly—my chest. It was tar black and drippy in the drain, but if I craned my neck I could spot the gray-light of some kind of opening a few feet ahead. *I was going to make it.*

Then one of the jagged bars poked my kidneys. I hissed and twisted away. Which was when my belt snagged.

I twisted back, but the bar jabbed me again like an oven poker. I groped in the muck for something to grab, to pull myself along. Nothing. I tried backing out, but my hands kept slipping. I took a deep breath and gave one good kick, hoping to squirt myself past the obstruction.

Red hot pain flashed in my side. The bar only dug deeper.

Forward, backward, rolling side to side... every move only hooked me tighter.

I told myself not to panic, but in less than a ten-count I was near flailing and splashing and ready to scream.

Wriggling in the stinky, slimy dark, the picture of a new cut headstone popped in my head. *Declan Flood*, it read. *He passed so young and died absurd—in the slop smellin' like a turd.*

I near screamed then, but bit my tongue. Over the wind, I heard grass rustling. Footsteps, coming my way.

Had the guards heard me writhing about? Were they smirking down at my legs right now, deciding whether to spear me or piss themselves laughing?

I froze, heart hammering in my chest. I swore I could hear its tiny echo off the stones around me.

The footsteps stopped. I lifted my head careful as can be and strained to hear anything.

A snort, then a laugh.

Bastards.

I was about to shout at the fookers to pull me out and at least kill me standing when Teagan's voice whispered out. "Why am I not surprised to find you down there?"

***

"Sweet Christ, you're rancid," Teagan said, passing me another towel.

I sponged gunk off my neck. "How did you get here?"

"Mayor Tom don't have the only horse in town, Declan." She squinted at me in the starlight. "He's right pissed, you know."

"No, I mean what are you doing *here*?" I demanded.

"Pulling your ungrateful arse out of the fire, apparently," she sniped.

We were standing in the shadow of a small horse cart loaded with vegetables. I gaped. Teagan began wiping my shoulders.

"Where'd this all come from?" I pointed, incredulous.

97

"My Ma's garden," she replied. "She's pissed, too."

The wind shifted suddenly, carried a bark of laughter, men talking. I flinched. The guards—

"Easy there, darlin'. Those two are fine. " She lifted the linen off a basket of sweet rolls. " I brought 'em these and apologized profusely, this order for her Majesty's larder coming so late."

I stared at Teagan. Moonbeams dimpled her chin and round cheeks. A coarse kitchen dress hung on her, fronted by a stained, frayed apron. The brim of the battered straw hat flopped in the wind, held on her head by a string under her chin. Her shawl and hair flapped to one side like ragged flags. She was the most beautiful thing I'd ever seen.

"How did you—?"

"Wasn't hard to work out, boyo. After we talked, I heard Paddy was the one who left with Meany, not you. And when the O'Meara boy said he saw you on the Mayor's horse, I put it together. Your Magalie's after the Queen Mother."

"She's not *mine*," I squawked.

She waved my objection off and fixed me with a hard look. Same look as her Ma. "You sure Paddy's in there?"

I swallowed. On the other side of the manor wall was King's own mother, Queen Niamh. More than likely, other high-born as well, along with dozens of attendants, and a troop of soldiers captained by a spleen-venting malignity named Odhran Kane.

And so was a simple soul snared into bearing the rancorous witchery of a vengeful ghost—my friend Paddy O' Doule. I was sure of it.

I nodded.

Teagan squared her shoulders. "Well, then, that's where we're going. Here." She hefted a large basket of turnips and greens into my arms. "You're helping me unload. Act slow-witted," she winked. "Shouldn't be too hard."

Together we walked through the servant's entrance.

***

Teagan led that horse and cart straight across the yard, marched into the kitchen like it was her own. In she went, dumping cabbages on the nearest table, reciting the perils of mud, tolls, thieving street brats and useless help—meaning me—before any of the staff knew what hit 'em. I shuffled in after, a bit of drool slipping out the corner of my mouth.

Four cooks, not one of them had ever laid eyes on her in their life, but she was so bold in belonging there, they believed it. Another minute, they were nodding and chuckling along with her.

"And this useless fella," she swopped me in the arm, "near let the wheels get pinched right off my cart. Put them there," she pointed me and my basket to the table.

"He's good for hefting, not much else," she whispered conspiratorially. "Fell out a tree when he was a wee lad." She rapped her knuckles on her head. "Ain't been the same since."

That earned a laugh.

"Oi!" she suddenly exclaimed at me. "You stepped in *something*."

She made a show of taking a big sniff, scrunched her face, then waved me out the door. "Outside with you. Wait. By. The. Cart."

She rolled her eyes and turned back to staff. "Sorry 'bout that. Doozy keeping track of him *all* the time. I'll bring the rest in myself."

I trotted out, head down, biting the inside of my cheek to keep from grinning.

Planting myself behind the bulk of the horse, I studied the royal residence. There had to be a way in.

The manor house was hunchback thick, with a squat center tower on one end, and a set of sharp roofs jutting like black saw-teeth at the stars. The first-floor windows close to me were bright, the curtains orange warm with firelight. Fuzzy figures moved behind them, rippling across the fabric like the shadows of clouds across a meadow.

The cook's entrance was twenty paces off; a dark arch of a doorway notched under a flat shed roof. My gaze drifted up the gable end to the oily shimmer of window glass on the second floor.

Paddy was looking down at me.

My heart stopped.

Without thinking, I grabbed a basket of vegetables and started walking.

The door was unlocked.

Heart in my mouth at the brass of it, I lifted the latch and slipped into in a tiny, dark pantry. I could make out shelves stacked with cutlery and crystal, the throat of a narrow hall leading further in. Ruddy light and noise murmured out of an open doorway midway down. At the far end, I spied the dull-dark-dull-dark accordion of stairs.

Letting out a breath I hadn't known I was holding, I moused forward, holding the basket in front of me like a shield. *Don't mind me,* I quavered in my head. *I'm just a stinky, dumb culchie, delivering to the wrong door.* A dozen creeps later the noise resolved: laughter, glasses tinkling, and a strumming cittern.

Queen Niamh was at supper.

Worming along the wall, I'd edged right up to the jamb when Kane's voice rang out. "I'll attend to him personally, your Majesty."

He snipped his words like spent blooms on a bush, a string of dead husks falling from his lips.

"Debts and lies come always paired," a woman said. "I want no further discussion until he pays."

Against my better judgment, I peeked around the corner.

Kane's back was to me, barely pissing distance away. Beyond him, a large dining room glittered with candlelight, crystal, and gilt. Kane was at attention, addressing the pair at the table.

The Queen Mother herself sat profile to me, wine glass in hand, posed for a portrait. Her beauty was aged, gray and stern as a rapier. She was staring at the man across the table, mouth dour.

The fellow was a balding old pudge with a red bulb nose and great woolly muttonchops. Wearing blue and gold silks, he had a nasty comb-over that made his head look like a duck egg clutched by a giant spider.

At her Majesty's words, he threw his head back and guffawed as if she'd made a great joke. "Words are the cheapest currency, your Majesty. But I fear the Earl of Connacht's treasury is full of little else." He winked and tossed back his wine. A servant darted in to refill his glass. I ducked back.

My jerkiness rattled the turnips and the whole fat dirty purple pile started to slide. I quick tucked the basket in and caught greens under my chin. Trembling, I slowly knelt and gently placed the wicker on the floor at my feet.

The Queen made some new comment, and it must have been the height of wit, because both the Old Baldy and Kane laughed. I peeked again; all three were still facing away.

Now or never.

Deep breath... and I shot past the doorway into the dark end of the hall.

At the foot of the stairs, the Queen's voice sounded behind me. "What *is* that horrid smell?"

"Not me!" Lord Pudge chuckled. "Stopped eating cabbage last year."

"I'll find out, your Majesty," Kane spoke over him.

I curled up as Odhran Kane strode into the hall. Instead of looking around, he turned toward the panty and promptly tripped over the basket. He caught himself and swore.

"Captain Kane?" the Queen Mother called out.

"It's nothing, your Majesty," he growled. "By your leave, I'll return momentarily." Without waiting for a reply, he snatched up a turnip and stomped toward the tiny pantry.

As I crept up the stairs, I heard Old Pudge behind me. "Bit odious, that man. Still," he tutted, "his type can be useful, don't you agree?"

"Absolutely," Queen Niamh replied.

Up I went.

The stairs joined another passage, this one wider with a long rug and a row of tall arched windows facing seaside. The candle sconces weren't lit, but starlight outlined ornate carved railings, brass fittings, even fancy painted paper on the wall. It hit me the glass panes alone in this house cost more than all of Carn earned in a year. I gaped.

Vicar Duffy always said if you want to know what God thinks of money, just look at the people He gives it to. Standing there, I finally understood what he meant.

It took all of two seconds to find Paddy. A bright sick light was smoldering under a door at the end of the hall, just like that night at Fades, like the light in Paddy's window.

I went in and found the both of them standing there. Paddy O' Doule and Magalie Morreaux, the Black Jewel of Senlis.

103

They stood in the middle of some kind of changing room with mirrors, little tables and curvy padded couches. Another fancy arched window took up most of the far wall. It was open to the wind and I could hear the crash and hiss of breakers boiling up from the rocks below.

They both turned to me. Paddy held the open locket. Beside him, Magalie was every inch the lost and lovely lass in the picture, only gauzy at the edges, like smoke. Her eyes met mine and she smiled triumphantly.

Paddy's face was creased. "You shouldn't have come, Dec."

"Paddy..." I croaked.

He shook his head. "You should go."

My mouth was dry ash. "I'm here to help. To bring you home."

Paddy looked questioningly at Magalie, then back at me. "I don't need your help no more, Dec. Magalie says so."

"Mate," I began. "Don't be heeding her. She's lying to you."

"No, no, no" he said. "I'm not listening. I don't have to no more. She says my finding things connects us. Makes me special."

Magalie started flickering, guttering like a candle; her dress, hair, face. One instant pretty, the next, the bloody *bean sí* of my dream. Smiling all the while. Paddy didn't seem to notice.

I tore my eyes off the stuttering nightmare and bulled ahead. "Paddy, she killed Fade—"

"'Cause he killed her," he snapped. "He sliced her and left her to drain like a pig in the dirt. It was wrong."

104

"Vengeance isn't ours to take. Ask her why she killed the Widow," I demanded. "She wasn't in the woods."

He stared at me stubbornly.

"Now she's after the Queen Mother," I explained. "To murder *her*. And you bringing her here paints you the same. Is that what you want?"

He thrust the locket toward me. The open lid flashed, the scratchy swirl of letters coiling like a tiny viper "I want you to leave me be," he pouted. "All you've ever done is use me: 'Paddy find me this' or 'Paddy where's my stuff?' All I'm good for is to get you money. You don't care about *me*."

It weren't all true, but enough of it was I staggered at the shame of it.

"Well, I don't need you no more," he declared. "Magalie says we can be together."

The skull-faced corpse girl grinned at me, bright red blood drenching her dress of laced fog and pyre smoke.

She touched his shoulder and spoke, her voice soft and dry as rotted silk, echoing across a great gulf. "It's time. Leave me open in her room. I will find you when it's done."

My blood chilled at that. She'd schemed him into some devilish compact. "Paddy," I started, "I never meant— "

"You never meant nothing," he replied gruffly.

That stung me. "Paddy, that's not true. I did mean it. You're my best mate. Have been since we were little. It never came out perfect, but you are. True as true."

105

He shoved past me. I grabbed him and he turned on me faster than an alley cat, face blooming into rage. "No. You aren't my friend. You're the same as the rest, calling me stupid, calling names."

He started punching me with his big ham fists, every word a blow. "No. More. No. More."

I went back and back until I hit the window sill. The ocean wind hummed in my ears, blew my hair.

My hands went up, but not fists. They clasped in front of me like a beggar. Like prayer. "She's poison, mate. Don't do it."

Paddy grabbed my shirt, hefted me up on my toes. His breath steamed in my face, the wind blasted my back. Glee was pouring off Magalie like heat off a coal stove. Waves shattered on the rocks below.

My eyes were shut, tears streaming down my cheeks. "Paddy, listen to me."

"Why?" he growled. A lurch. Cold open sky behind me.

"Because I'm sorry."

"That it?"

"It's all I got. I'm out of words, out of excuses, out of smart-ass things to say. All I got is sorry from the bottom of my heart."

A pause. "You were gonna come to Daire with Meany. Why?"

"I wanted to pawn that thing for whatever I could." I said miserably. "Get it far away from Carn."

"But I had the locket," Paddy said. "Why'd you still come?"

"Because... Because you're my friend. Because you're all I have left and I can't stand—" I choked. "I can't stand the thought of death taking you, too."

My boots swayed, then touched floorboard. I opened my eyes to see Paddy glaring down at me. "You mean that?"

I nodded.

Paddy turned to Magalie. The pale princess of Senlis glided forward, worry etched across porcelain features. She opened her mouth to speak.

"Don't." Paddy held up the open locket. "You said all he cared about was money. That he wouldn't follow after."

"Jealousy," her withered voice insisted. "That one envies what we have. What we *will have* after. A new life, a new home—"

Paddy scrunched his brow, looked from the locket to her and back to the locket. Then gazed around the room as if seeing it for the first time.

"No," he said slowly. "I already got a home."

With that, he snapped the locket shut and in one smooth motion turned and flung it past my head, out the window, far into the surging sea.

Neither of us uttered a word. The wind gusted, the waves roared, but in that stunned moment, I swear I heard a scream.

It took a bit but after a long minute, I looked at Paddy and where we were standing and said, "We have to get out of here."

"I know a way out," Paddy said.

We started for the door. "Teagan's here," I whispered. "We gotta find her."

He smiled and nodded. "Righto. Finding things is what I do."

***

I bought a ring out of Fade's glass case when they auctioned off his estate. The whole town was there and Mayor Tom presided. I got a good deal on account of there being no other bids on that particular item.

Vicar Duffy said the blessings over us, and I took up helping Teagan mind the inn. Eighteen months later, she had our first child, a boy.

We named him Paddy.

Epilogue – The Waves Roll on

The waters at the mouth of the harbor were contrary, the ocean sending ugly green and gray waves to batter their boat while the winds whipped up whitecaps and spray cold as snow.

The older man with the orange cap and face like a hunk of driftwood bent double over the gunnels. The second man, younger, with a wispy beard he thought made him look older, sat on the bench beside him. Around their boots swirled a slime of sick and sea-scum. Mounds of rope net and empty wicker baskets were lumped evenly along the port and starboard sides.

"Put your back into it, Garrit. I can't do it all myself," the older man rasped.

The young man blushed, and burped back the sourness in his throat. "Sorry, Ferg. I's watching the horizon like you said." He leaned over and grabbed a handful of net. "You know, no matter how long you stare though, you can't exact line up where the sea and sky meet.

The waves roll on and on, right up into the clouds if you ask me. It's like they're rooted in each other."

"Fookin' poet are you?" The older man eyed him skeptically. "You know what I see?"

"No, Ferg."

"I see empty nets and empty creel, which means empty bellies and empty pockets. Now pull, damn you, and pray we get a catch."

The two of them hauled the slick freezing hemp one heave at a time into their boat. It spilled across the bottom, a slithering mass of gunk, seaweed, and the occasional pale gleam of wriggling fish scales.

Fergus rattled out what passed for a sigh. "Untangle this mess, creel anything with fins. We're not throwing back today."

They spent the next half hour in silence save the slap of waves, the scouring rush of winds. Fingers numb beyond feeling, Garrit was fumbling with a particularly grisly knot when he felt something smooth and heavy as a clamshell.

He pried it out between two lengths of rope and wiped it on his pants. Yellow gleamed through the muck. "Here, Ferg. Look at this."

Fergus turned, expecting another twist of driftwood or some odd shell had fascinated the young man once again. Garrit wiped it more, held up a shiny disc between his finger and thumb.

"That looks like—" Fergus began.

"Gold," Garrit finished. "Viking treasure, you think?"

"What are you quizzing me for?" Fergus groused. "You were the one reading books."

Garrit pulled a rag out of his jacket pocket and began rubbing. "It's jewelry. Looks like...letters." He ran his finger around the edge, prying off a string of mermaid hair, and the top popped up slightly.

Garrit teased the lid up and stared. "Will you look at that," he breathed out.

THE END

Special Thanks and Author's Note

Gratitude as always to The Fortnighters for nudging the luck o' the Irish on this yarn, to Michal Oracz for another excellent cover, to Jim at Panera for the good cheer and occasional free carbs, to Glynda Francis for tidying up after me. Thank you.

Readers, if you're looking for historical accuracy, please stop. Writing this, I pilfered five centuries of Celtic history, place-names and terms. Declan and Paddy's Eire is a fictional, mythical place that exists nowhere save my precarious imagination. I went with what felt right, sounded right, and I plead poetic license. I beg your indulgence and hope you found your time with them well spent. A thousand thanks.

Patrick Todoroff - Autumn 2014
SDG